A PONY called SECRET

A Friend in Need

OLIVIA TUFFIN

nosy
crow

For my wonderful parents, who have
always believed in my stories.

First published in the UK in 2018 by Nosy Crow Ltd
The Crow's Nest, 14 Baden Place
Crosby Row, London SE1 1YW
www.nosycrow.com

ISBN: 978 1 78800 027 7

Nosy Crow and associated logos are trademarks
and/or registered trademarks of Nosy Crow Ltd

Text © Olivia Tuffin 2018
Pony photographs © Matthew Bishop Photography 2018

The right of Olivia Tuffin to be identified as the author has been asserted.

All rights reserved

This book is sold subject to the condition that it shall not,
by way of trade or otherwise, be lent, hired out or otherwise circulated in
any form of binding or cover other than that in which it is published.
No part of this publication may be reproduced, stored in a retrieval system,
or transmitted in any form or by any means
(electronic, mechanical, photocopying, recording or otherwise)
without the prior written permission of Nosy Crow Ltd.

A CIP catalogue record for this book is available from the British Library.

Printed and bound in the UK by Clays Ltd, St Ives Plc.
Typeset by Tiger Media

Papers used by Nosy Crow are made from wood grown in
sustainable forests.

1 3 5 7 9 8 6 4 2

PROLOGUE

Alice pushed open the door to the spare room and headed straight to the bookshelves. There were so many pony books that she felt sure there must be one about training tricky ponies!

As she touched each book spine in turn, Alice's eyes were drawn to a scrapbook stuffed in behind the other books. Pulling it out, she smiled as she spotted a photo of her mum as a teenager.

Josephine was sailing over a jump with a determined look on her face. It was strange for Alice to see her mum on a horse as she hadn't ridden in years.

The pony in all the photos was a gorgeous grey. Alice recognised him as Master Blue, her mum's beloved pony who had died when Alice was just a baby. Alice traced the words with her fingers as she read about success after success. Flicking to the last few pages, Alice felt a lump rise in her throat.

Here was Blue in a veterinary hospital, her mum lying next to her pony as they slept side by side. A vet's notes had been stuck in next to the photo. One part stood out to Alice. *'Severe damage to the deep digital flexor tendon. Prognosis poor.'*

Alice turned the page. Here the words were scrawled on the page with such force the ink had splattered.

A PONY called SECRET

Angus persuaded me to ride to the beach. Why did he just gallop off? Why didn't he stop? WHY did he think he was helping me? Blue will never be ridden again. Angus has ruined EVERYTHING.

Alice could feel her mum's anger radiating from the page. She quickly closed the scrapbook. What had happened to Master Blue? Was Angus, Finn's dad, really to blame? And what did all this mean for Alice and Finn…?

Chapter 1

"Well, that wasn't our best." Alice reached down and patted Secret, her roan pony, as she walked him back up to the yard on a loose rein. "I'm sorry if I let you down, boy."

It was late afternoon on a freezing cold New Year's Eve and Alice had just returned from a jumping session in the outdoor school. Fergus, the head groom, had helped her set up a small course.

Secret had almost cleared the lot in one leap, his scope incredible for a small pony. With his ears pricked and a merry spring in his canter, it had taken all of Alice's strength to stop him jumping straight out over the arena fence. And the more she held him back, the more erratic his jumping style became, taking off several strides early and then charging on to the next fence.

"What do I do?" Alice had said helplessly to Fergus.

Fergus had smiled kindly. "Well, he's definitely keen. Let's just hope they have a decent jumping instructor at the pony club!"

Alice untacked Secret with numb fingers and put his rug back on before leading him into his stable, the shelter a relief from the icy wind. Secret immediately started to tuck into his hay net, and Alice smiled, leaning against him for a few moments. Although Secret was a purebred

Section B, and perfectly capable of living out in the cold, Alice was glad he was in his cosy stable.

Fergus chuckled. "You'd have that pony living in your bedroom if you could. If he was on a Welsh mountain, he'd have to survive outside!"

Alice grinned. "I know, but he's so used to his creature comforts now I can't make him go outside in this." Then she laughed as Secret butted her gently as if in agreement before turning back to his hay.

"Pfft. Spoilt boy."

Alice knew Fergus was only teasing her. All the ponies in her mum's showing yard were in at night, even the hardy breeds like Porridge the Shetland and Lachlan the Highland. The winter had already been long and hard and summer seemed like a lifetime ago.

"I'll tell you who must be finding it tough…"

Fergus leaned on the door. "Finn and Sasha's new mare. Poor thing, coming from Spain to a harsh British winter. Finn probably *has* got her inside the house, knowing him."

Alice's tummy flipped at the mention of Finn. "I wouldn't know what Finn is up to nowadays," she muttered, concentrating hard on her pony.

Fourteen-year-old Finn Cutler and his older sister, Sasha, had spent lots of time with Alice and her family over the summer. Finn had ridden the yard's show ponies alongside performing in the Flying Fillies, his family's amazing pony display team. Alice and Finn had become really close, and she'd thought they had a special bond.

But then Finn's dad had arrived back after more than a year working away and Alice had barely seen Finn since. It turned out that Finn's dad, Angus, and Alice's mum, Josephine, knew each other from way back, and they *really* didn't like each other. Alice knew their disagreement was connected to her mum's old horse, Master Blue, and after finding the scrapbook she knew that her mum held Angus responsible for Blue's accident. Alice longed to know exactly what had happened but her mum refused to talk about it. And since Angus's return they'd barely seen or heard from Finn. He'd even pulled out of riding at the Horse of the Year Show with Alice, choosing instead to go to Spain with his dad to rescue a pony.

Playing with Secret's forelock, Alice thought back to the summer. Finn had been the first person she had confided in about her problems with Secret. The little red pony had been a challenge from the start, wilful and hot-headed. Although he and Alice adored each other, and Alice was a great rider, she struggled with him at times. Since she had stopped showing him things had improved, but Alice missed Finn's help and advice. He had

A PONY called SECRET

an amazing way with horses and was an incredible rider.

Trying to shake Finn from her thoughts, Alice sighed. Anyway, she'd be seeing him soon enough. She had finally joined the pony club, and most of the winter programme was to be held at Hilltops, an equestrian centre just four miles away. Tomorrow, on New Year's Day, Alice was going to her first event. And the Flying Fillies, Finn and Sasha's pony display team, were going to be putting on a show.

On the one hand, Alice couldn't wait; it was a chance to get to know everyone and have her first taste of pony club life. But it would be the first time she had seen Finn in months, and she couldn't stop the butterflies in her stomach from fluttering. Well, not so much fluttering as banging and crashing into each other! Alice felt sick. Would Finn still look the same and act the same towards her?

★

Later that night, as the clock crept closer to midnight, Alice decided to go and say a final goodnight to Secret. Her mum and dad were watching the New Year's Eve celebrations on the TV in the living room. Pulling a bobble hat on over her pale hair, Alice slipped and slid down the garden path. There was no need for a torch as the moon was incredibly bright, bathing the garden and yard in a silvery light. There were a thousand stars overhead and everything was frozen solid and still. A few of the ponies were lying down, blinking sleepily at Alice as she passed the stables. And there, at the end of the line, was Secret. He was resting a leg, his eyes shut, but on hearing Alice's footsteps he gave a whicker.

Opening the stable door, Alice smiled. "Nearly the new year, my boy. A big year for us."

It seemed amazing to think that a year ago Alice

had ridden Secret for the first time. It hadn't been an easy few months. Despite Alice's mum being a very well-known showing producer, it became clear after several disastrous events that the young and feisty Secret wasn't cut out for the show ring. Alice had finally decided that he – and she – would be better suited to jumping.

But things weren't straightforward with the jumping either. Secret had raw talent, but Alice didn't know how to move forward with him.

As Secret sank down into his bed, Alice put her arms round him. Over the still night air, she could just hear the church bells chime midnight, the deep tones floating up to Park Farm, along with the faintest sounds of cheering and 'Auld Lang Syne'. Alice hadn't had any party invites, never having enough time to see friends from school. But it was much better being here with Secret. Giving him a final hug, she stretched her long legs, now stiff with cold, as she got up. Who knew what the new year had in store for her and her mischievous pony!

Chapter 2

"You must be Alice Smalley!"

No sooner had Alice and her mum entered the equestrian centre than Alice found her hand grasped in a firm handshake by June Darby, the district commissioner of Hilltops pony club. Alice had heard June was kind but didn't take any nonsense. With her steely blue eyes and brisk voice, Alice could well believe that. She hid a smile, wondering what June would think of Secret and his naughty ways!

"We've been looking forward to meeting you both," June continued. "We've got plenty planned for this coming year. What is it you really like doing?"

Alice felt put on the spot. "Um, I like showjumping. We've been jumping some small courses." It sounded a bit silly when she said it like that; she and Secret had only recently been jumping in their school at home.

"Wonderful!" June clapped her hands together. "We're putting together a junior showjumping team. It's the one team that is a little thin on the ground but I'm hoping that will change this year. We've got big plans for it: regular training, area competitions, that sort of thing."

Alice smiled at the older woman. She felt a bubble of excitement rise at the thought of a

possible place on the team. She'd love for her and Secret to make friends and receive regular feedback, as well as have the chance to compete against other teams.

There were plenty of people milling around, and tables laden with party food. Everyone seemed to know each other, and talked confidently about ponies and their Christmas holidays. Alice's mum was soon chatting to someone, while Alice hovered next to the food, hoping to find someone she could talk to. She couldn't help but look around for Finn, but there was no sign of him.

"Hi!"

Alice jumped as a girl appeared next to her, a friendly smile on her face. She was incredibly pretty, with dark glossy hair tied in a ponytail and huge green eyes framed by long dark eyelashes. She reminded Alice of a well-groomed cat.

"I'm Hannah," the girl said.

"Hi, Hannah," Alice said a little shyly. "I'm Alice. I'm new."

"I guessed," Hannah said, raising an eyebrow. "Or you'd have helped yourself to all the best food!"

Alice laughed, feeling herself relax.

"So you're local?" Hannah questioned. "I heard we had a new member. Why didn't you join until now?"

Alice thought about her answer. She *had* been about to join the pony club just before her old pony Honey's accident. But she didn't want to go into that now. Without thinking she touched the scar on her cheek, a reminder of that awful day, and wondered if Hannah had noticed it. The scar had faded, but Alice was very conscious of it. "I'm really busy normally, helping my mum; she's over there." She gestured at Josephine, who was deep in conversation. "She runs a showing yard but

I've got my own pony now, a Welsh Section B, and we're going to do our own thing."

"Cool," Hannah said. "I love Section Bs."

"Are you local too?" Alice asked, grabbing a handful of crisps.

"You could say that!" Hannah laughed. "I live here."

"What, here?" Alice looked round her.

"Well, obviously not in the stables!" Hannah looked at her in amusement. "But, yeah, we live here. My dad runs the livery yard and most of the group lessons are held here. It means I get to know *everyone* horsey."

Alice smiled. Hannah seemed very confident. Alice wished she could be more like that!

A group of people came into the room and Hannah waved them over.

"Alice, this is Lola, Rosie, Jordan, Amy and Sam. They'll be in your ride with me. How old are you?"

"Thirteen," Alice said, smiling and trying to remember their names as they gathered around her. Everyone seemed to gravitate towards Hannah, asking her about her Christmas and New Year's Eve. It seemed Hannah had been to some glamorous party in London and all the girls listened intently as Hannah filled them in on the night's events. Alice thought about her own New Year's Eve, sitting in the straw in Secret's stable.

"Hi, Alice." Jordan, one of two boys, gave her a wave. He was nice-looking with light brown hair and hazel eyes. "We're *the* most popular boys in the pony club."

"That's because you're the *only* boys in the branch," Hannah said, arching one beautifully shaped eyebrow.

Jordan laughed. "Ah, you spoil all the fun, Hannah."

Hannah linked arms with Alice. "Come and sit

with us," she said, pulling Alice away.

Alice glanced over at her mum, who was still talking, and gave her a wave to let her know she was going to go and sit with her new friends. She thought it was unlikely her mum was going to watch the display.

"So, this display is exciting, isn't it? How gorgeous is Finn?"

Alice looked up sharply. How did Hannah know Finn?

"Oooh, Hannah, has he been in touch?" Lola giggled and Hannah smiled a confident, knowing smile.

"Texted me this morning." she said in a smug voice.

"How do you know Finn?" Alice was finally able to get her words out.

Hannah turned to her as they took their seats. "Oh, do you know him as well?"

19

Alice nodded. Suddenly she felt the need to prove to Hannah that she and Finn were friends.

"Yes," she said in what she hoped was a confident voice. "I know him well actually. He rode ponies for my mum last summer."

"I see." Hannah narrowed her green eyes a little as she looked at Alice. "So, do you see him loads?"

Alice hesitated. "Well, not recently."

"He came around with his dad last week," Hannah said, a small smile on her lips. "He's so nice, isn't he? Funny and cheerful."

Alice frowned. That didn't sound like the Finn she knew. He *was* funny, but he kept his guard up, and she certainly wouldn't describe him as cheerful.

"So, do you think he has a girlfriend?" Hannah said, looking straight at Alice. "I mean, *look* at him!"

Alice wavered for a moment. "Er, no. No, I don't

think he does."

"But how do you *know*?" Hannah pressed. "You said you hadn't seen him recently."

Alice opened her mouth, and then closed it again, unable to think of a reply. Her mind was whirring. Why had Finn and Angus been visiting the equestrian centre?

"Hannah, you HAVE to invite Finn to your party!" Lola squealed. "How's the planning coming along?"

"I already did, and it's going to be *amazing*," Hannah said. "Dad's managed to get a DJ to come up from a London club. Normally he wouldn't do fourteenth birthday parties, but he said he would, for me."

Alice sat awkwardly as Hannah talked across her, telling everyone about the Winter Wonderland party that would be held in February for her birthday.

"Soooo many people are coming," she continued. "Loads of people from pony club and school."

Amy nudged Hannah and glanced quickly at Alice. Hannah followed her gaze. "Oh, Alice, you must come along too!" she added. "'I'll get an invite to you."

Alice smiled and nodded, although she couldn't help thinking that Hannah didn't sound very sincere. Perhaps she was just imagining things.

Soon any further chatting was halted as the lights dimmed and a spotlight fell on the arena. An excited buzz filled the seating area, which was completely full. The first bars of the music Alice knew so well rang out, and she felt the hairs on her arms stand up. The last time she had heard this music had been at a party held by Samantha, a client of Josephine's. Alice and Secret had performed with the team, and it had been a real turning point in their relationship. Inexplicably

her eyes filled with tears and she quickly brushed them away.

The spotlight fell on Sasha, Finn's older sister, and her beautiful grey, Robin. Alice had got to know the horses at Finn's yard over the summer and she missed them so much.

The crowd were cheering now, as Robin reared higher and higher in the spotlight, Sasha never moving from her side saddle. Then in came Molly standing astride the back of the two Dales ponies, Jack and Jill. Alice had ridden Jill at the party in the summer. She felt a stab of jealousy. It wasn't that she wanted to ride in the team like Molly; she just wanted to be involved somehow.

Next a rider galloped in on the chestnut ex racehorse Marcus used to ride. Marcus was Sasha's horrible ex-boyfriend. He used to ride for the team before he was fired. The new boy was a brilliant rider, throwing himself off the side of his horse in the blink of an eye. The pony club members, nearly all of whom were girls, gasped and cheered as the fourth rider rode in on the most beautiful snow white Highland. It was Finn on his pony Horatio, and Alice felt her stomach turn over.

"Oh Hannah!" Lola gasped. "He's sooooo gorgeous! He'd better accept your party invitation."

"Oh, I'm sure he will," Hannah grinned, never taking her eyes away from him.

Alice bit her cheek and said nothing, trying to concentrate on the performance. She knew practically every move in the Flying Fillies' routine. As Finn cantered past, waving to the crowd, Alice wondered if he'd seen her. It was as if the whole previous summer had never happened, and she was back to watching the Flying Fillies after her show classes, wondering if the dark-haired boy ever noticed her watching.

Chapter 3

"Amazing!" Hannah cried as the Flying Fillies cantered around the arena one final time, waving and laughing. "Can you imagine June's face if we all wanted to try that instead of boring dressage. Hilarious! Maybe Angus will teach us some moves in his lessons."

"So Angus is definitely the new instructor?" Jordan asked Hannah, who nodded.

"*Angus* is coming to teach here?" Alice gasped before she could stop herself, as Hannah raised a surprised eyebrow.

"Yep," she explained. "He'll be concentrating on getting the showjumping team back off the ground again. My dad put a word in for him."

Alice tried to smile along with the others, but her mind was whirring. Would her mum even let her join the pony club if Angus was going to teach? Alice thought back to the scrapbook and her mum's bitter words blaming Angus for Blue's injury. Was Alice's new dream over before it had even started?

As soon as the show was over, Alice slipped off quietly from Hannah and the rest of the group. After seeing Finn in the show, she just wanted to chat to him. Taking a deep breath, she walked round to the Flying Fillies' lorry. Finn and Sasha

were rugging their horses up, the atmosphere cheerful. Alice hugged her coat round her as she approached, just as Finn turned and gave a start. For a second, as their eyes met, Alice felt a spark before Finn smiled.

"Hey, Alice."

"Hey," Alice mumbled. Finn looked different. Happier, more relaxed. Maybe Hannah *was* right, maybe he was cheerful. Or maybe he was just cheerful with Hannah. She shook the thought from her mind.

"Are you involved with the pony club at last?" Finn asked, and Alice nodded. "How is my favourite red pony?"

Alice didn't know quite what to say, even though she had plenty she *wanted* to say. After a summer of seeing each other all the time, Finn had basically walked out of her life, and she wanted to know why.

Seeming to sense her mood, Finn turned to Sasha. "Sash, can you look after things here for a minute? I want to catch up with Alice."

"Course. Hi, Alice!" The older girl gave Alice a friendly smile and she waved shyly back. She was still slightly in awe of the effortlessly glamorous Sasha.

Turning to Alice, Finn pointed towards a stable block to the left of the arena. "Come on, let's get out of the cold."

Alice tried not to think about the fact that Finn knew his way around already, but it was a relief to get out of the biting wind. Sitting on a hay bale, Finn gestured for Alice to do the same. She sat down cautiously. Finn seemed so … grown up.

"So," she began, just as Finn started to talk. They both laughed a little awkwardly.

Finn smiled. "Go on."

"I just wondered what's going on," Alice

blurted out. "You seemed to enjoy working with Mum. I thought you'd be at the Horse of the Year Show after everything…" *And what about me!* she added in her head.

"I knew you'd be OK. You ride the ponies brilliantly," Finn said. "Dad really needed my help in Spain. And anyway—" he paused —"I didn't think your mum really wanted me around any more."

"How could you know that?" Alice cried, ignoring Finn's compliment and feeling anger rise up inside her. "You didn't even bother to get in touch. You said you'd text me… You said you wanted to see how I did with Secret…" She hadn't meant for it all to come out in a big rush.

"I *am* sorry," Finn said. "I just had all kinds of stuff going on, like with my dad coming back and the new pony. She's taken up loads of time."

Alice took a deep breath, trying to see things

from Finn's point of view. "Tell me more about the new pony," she said after a pause.

Finn's face lit up. "She's amazing," he said. "She's come so far in such a short space of time. I'm getting there, slowly."

As he spoke, lost in his own world, Alice felt her tummy flutter at the deep connection Finn had with horses.

"Dad was the one who rescued her, but she seems to prefer me," Finn continued. "So she's my special project. Our horses are on holiday from now until spring, so I can spend lots of time with her."

"I'd love to meet her," Alice said sincerely.

Finn smiled. "I'd like that."

Sitting there with Finn, Alice forgot all about Hannah's comments and the months that had passed. It was just her and Finn again, like it used to be.

"Are you still going to ride for my mum?" Alice asked, mentally crossing her fingers.

"Well," Finn said. "Samantha has asked me to ride Archie again. If your mum's here now, I can ask her if she thinks that might work out."

Jumping up, Finn reached down to pull Alice up, her freezing cold hand in his. His hands were equally cold, but Alice's seemed to burn in Finn's grasp. They both quickly dropped their hands to their sides.

As they crossed the yard Alice thought back to the last time her mum had spoken to Finn, at Samantha's party when Angus had returned. Remembering her mum's scrapbook entry, she tried to connect the Angus her mum had written about, who had played a part in Blue's catastrophic injury, to the man who had gone back to Spain to rescue a pony.

As Finn opened the doors, Alice was aware that

Hannah was staring intently at them both.

Her mum gave a start of surprise as she spotted Finn. "Hello, Finn," Josephine said with a thin smile. "Sounds like it was a great show."

"Thanks."

There was an awkward silence as Josephine waited for Finn to continue.

"I'm sorry I wasn't able to ride at the Horse of the Year Show," Finn said sincerely. "It's just that with everything going on…"

"It was disappointing," Alice's mum said briskly.

"I would've loved to have ridden," Finn continued, stumbling a little on his words, "but Dad needed my help."

"Of course. *Angus* needed you." Alice's mum frowned and she shook her head. "I can't believe I never realised you were his son," she said. "You look so much like him."

"If you had realised who my dad was, you'd

never have given me a chance," Finn said quietly.

Josephine sighed. "You're right," she said. "It was a shock seeing him after all these years. When I knew him he lived up north. I never expected to see him again…" Josephine looked as though she was going to say something else, and then stopped herself. "Well, as you know, Samantha has asked if you can be Archie's main rider this season. He's not coming back for a few weeks, so shall we discuss a schedule nearer the time?"

"I'd like that," Finn said.

Josephine nodded. "Excellent. And will your father be happy with this arrangement?"

Finn shrugged. "As long as I've got time for everything else: the displays and the mare's rehab."

"And will you let me know if your father decides to whisk you away somewhere just before an important show?" Josephine said, her voice bitter again.

"He's here to stay," Finn said, looking at Alice. "What with the Flying Fillies and the new pony and everything."

"And my new teaching job."

Angus had appeared behind his son. His eyes and hair were as dark as Finn's. Immediately the atmosphere shifted: tension crackling in the air.

Josephine folded her arms. "Teaching where?" she snapped as Alice held her breath.

"Here," Angus said calmly. "I'll be running the showjumping lessons."

Josephine's mouth dropped open.

"It'll be nice to see you back at a showjumping arena, Josie, if Alice comes along," Angus continued.

"I've stayed away from showjumping for many years," Josephine replied in an icy voice. "Ever since Blue."

Angus gazed at her. "I still feel guilty about Blue

every day," he said quietly.

"Oh!" Josephine laughed bitterly. "I always thought you were too arrogant to feel guilt."

Angus's eyes grew blacker, and his hands clenched and unclenched, just as Finn's did when he was wound up. Alice cleared her throat, hoping to diffuse the tension, and Angus gave a start as if noticing she was there for the first time.

"Finn's been raving about Secret," he said to her warmly, and Alice couldn't help but feel pleased, imagining Finn talking about her with his dad.

"I've been jumping him recently," Alice blurted out. "His scope is amazing but I need help. He can get a bit … uncontrollable."

"He sounds great," Angus said. "I like a challenge. Sounds like you just need to let go and trust him."

Alice was suddenly aware of her mum. She looked furious.

"'Let go'?" she said, her voice dangerously quiet.

Angus frowned. "Josie, I'd never put Alice or Secret in danger."

"'Let go'?" Josephine repeated, louder this time. "Where have I heard that before? Was it when *I* trusted you and took your advice?"

Her voice was shrill now, attracting attention.

"Josie—" Angus's voice was quiet, level —"I will never forget what happened that day. I thought I was doing the right thing. I was young, like you, and I'm sorry."

"The right thing?" Josephine laughed bitterly. "Your 'right thing' cost me my confidence, my pony's career, and nearly his life! How can I trust you with my daughter and her pony?"

"But my son rides for you," Angus said, "so we're going to have to get along somehow."

"Do we?" Alice's mum retorted. "How do I know you're responsible now? Running off to

Spain, leaving poor Finn and Sasha to fend for themselves…"

"You know nothing about that," Angus replied, his eyes black.

Alice was aware that the room had grown quiet as everyone, including Hannah and her friends, watched the argument with open mouths. Alice felt herself redden to the roots of her pale hair and willed the floor to open up underneath her.

Finn just stared blankly ahead.

Josephine glared at Angus, lowering her voice. "I'll be watching you, Angus," she said coldly. "Come on, Alice. Goodbye, Finn."

She was stopped by June Darby, who was just coming into the room and picked up on the tension.

"All OK?" she asked, raising an eyebrow.

"Fine, thank you." Josephine seemed calm again, and she made polite conversation with her. Alice hovered next to her, trying not to make eye contact with anyone, but aware that Hannah was gliding across the room towards Finn. Alice watched as Hannah hugged Angus and then Finn, who actually hugged her back.

"So nice to see you both again," Hannah said in a tinkly voice. "I'm so excited about *everything*!"

As she spoke, her eyes met Alice's, and she smiled a cool, satisfied smile that didn't reach her eyes. Then Alice's mum tapped Alice on the arm, gesturing that it was time to go. It felt as though everyone in the room was watching them leave, and as Alice pushed open the doors, the icy air hitting her hot, red face, Hannah's laugh rang in her ears.

Chapter 4

"What happened, Mum? How exactly is it Angus's fault that Blue got injured?"

Back at home a few hours later, Alice was still burning with embarrassment following the argument at the equestrian centre. She had to know what had happened all those years before.

Josephine was sitting in the kitchen with a cup of tea. She gazed out of the window across the yard, and sighed deeply.

"Because Angus thought he knew what was best, for Blue and me," she said flatly. "It turned out he didn't."

Alice waited for her mum to continue.

"Angus and I were on the same showjumping team, and we were at a competition in the north," Josephine said quietly. "Blue and I were having problems. We weren't gelling, getting our striding wrong, making silly mistakes. He was hot-headed and tricky, but it made him the jumper he was. I was getting frustrated. Angus said I was putting too much pressure on both Blue and me as a partnership."

Just like Secret and me last year, Alice thought. Finn had pointed out the same thing then.

"Mum, I found your scrapbook," Alice said quietly, as her mum looked up sharply. "I know something happened at the beach. But what?"

A PONY called SECRET

Her mum sighed again and rubbed her eyes. "Angus persuaded me to take Blue down to the beach early one morning with him," she said finally. "I knew Blue would find it too much. He was nervy and flighty – it was part of the reason why he was so good: no one could catch him in a jump-off – but Angus took his ponies to the beach every morning to relax them, and he was doing so well, I thought I would give it a go. Angus had a way about him, and I believed him."

It was as if Alice was no longer there as her mum continued in the same flat tone.

"I knew it was a bad idea from the start. I should have stopped … said something. The waves were huge. Angus was laughing and just said to 'let him go', that he'd relax when he'd had a run. He set off, no tack, just laughing at me. He always could ride well. I remember it so clearly, the way he turned round, telling me to let Blue go."

Alice could picture the scene. A storm-lashed beach, a dark-haired boy just like Finn, arrogant in his confidence. And her mum, clinging on to a pony. She shivered.

"Blue got spooked and bolted straight for the sea but he tripped where the sand was shifting, and went over. I don't remember much after that."

Alice was silent, imagining the scene.

"I was unconscious, but I was told that Blue was on the verge of being shot there and then on the beach because they thought he'd broken a leg," Josephine continued. "Angus persuaded the vets to take him to the hospital because he suspected it was the tendon. I owe him that, at least. Blue could never be ridden again – you must have seen the vet's report. And I nearly gave it all up as well. I haven't really ridden since. I tell people I prefer to concentrate on the groundwork instead. But the real reason is that I totally lost my confidence."

"Oh, Mum."

There was nothing more Alice could say. She understood now why her mum had been so upset about seeing Angus again. It must have brought everything back. But no one had forced her to ride Blue down on the beach.

Alice frowned. "Mum," she started carefully, "Angus must have thought he was doing the right thing. Finn told me he adores horses."

Pain flashed over her mum's face. "Angus didn't plan to injure Blue," she said softly, "but he *always* thinks that his way is the right way. Don't you see why I'm worried about him being at the pony club? What if something happened to Secret? Or you?"

"It won't, Mum! Secret and I are different." Alice reached out to her mum and held her hand. "You need to trust us."

Her mum gave a shaky smile and squeezed Alice's hand, before heading into the yard. Alice breathed out deeply. What a mess. She could see what Angus had been trying to do. He loved horses, just like Finn. She felt torn in two directions: loyalty to her mum, and her desire to succeed with Secret.

★

Nothing was mentioned about Angus or the pony club for a few days. But then one afternoon Josephine leaned on the arena fence watching as Alice jumped. Secret had flown over the fences, ears pricked and eyes bright, and despite feeling slightly out of control Alice was laughing joyfully as she pulled Secret up and gave him a pat. It felt brilliant when it went well. No sign of the bored pony from the show ring!

Alice was pleased that her mum had caught one of her and Secret's more successful sessions. Unlike the previous week, when Secret had jumped Alice clean out of the saddle.

"What about trying a competition next week?" her mum suggested. "They hold fun shows at Hilltops, as well as pony club stuff. We'll start small: you can just trot around."

"OK," Alice agreed, pleased her mum was encouraging her jumping. Then she frowned as her mum continued.

"I asked the district commissioner of the Purley branch of the pony club if you could join there, since we almost overlap areas," her mum said casually, not quite meeting Alice's eyes. "They said that's fine. After all, it doesn't matter what branch you join."

Alice saw red. The Purley branch was further away, but it wasn't just that. What about Finn, and all the people she'd met on New Year's Day? She knew it was going to be hard, going back and facing everyone after Angus and her mum's argument, but she was determined to make it work.

"Yes, it does matter!" she cried, making Secret jump. "I want to be part of the *local* pony club, Hilltops! I never have time to see friends from school so I want to be part of something right here, and make some *proper* friends."

"OK, Alice, calm down. We'll enter the showjumping for now, and I'll talk about branches when you're not so wound up," her mum snapped, and Alice could tell she'd touched a nerve. Her mum had apologised more than once in the past for Alice missing school parties and get-togethers due to the busy show season. Alice decided she would use this to her advantage.

"And I want to do lessons! Proper group lessons, locally. With the chance to get into a team," she continued, emotion flooding through her. "It's great riding here, with you, but this is our chance to do something new!"

"All right!" Her mum held her hands up. "It was

only a suggestion. But, Alice, remember what I said… I'll be keeping a close eye on Angus." Her words hung in the air as she strode away, a dark frown on her face.

★

The day before the novice class at the equestrian centre Alice was bubbling with excitement, thinking about jumping Secret. She hadn't felt like that about a competitive event for a long time. However, her excitement was tinged with nerves. Most of the pony club members would be there, and Alice would have to face them all. But, more importantly, Finn and his dad would be there.

It was freezing cold, and riding under bare trees silhouetted against an iron-grey sky, Alice thought back to the summer and sighed as she passed the sign to the bridleway that led to the downs. She often thought about the ride she had had with Finn there, cantering along side by side, jumping the log with Finn's encouragement. It was when she had realised what Secret had been trying to tell her, that he didn't enjoy showing. That ride had been such a turning point in their relationship, both with Secret, and with Finn.

Chapter 5

There was a familiar four-by-four in the yard as Alice clattered back through the gates. Samantha! She must be visiting Josephine to discuss her ponies' return to Park Farm.

Samantha crossed the yard to give Alice a hug as she finished untacking Secret.

"It's so great that Finn's coming back to ride this summer. He's got such a bond with Archie,"

Samantha said, beaming. "Isn't it super?"

"Yes, it's great." Alice tried to look casual, but blushed as she noticed Samantha smiling.

"I'm actually going over to his house after this," Samantha continued. "Want to come?"

Alice longed to see the new Spanish mare, as well as Finn.

"Yes please!" she answered quickly.

"Perfect!" Samantha winked. "I'll just let your mum know we're heading over there and then we'll go as soon as you have Secret turned out in his field."

"Great!" Alice said happily, knowing that her mum would be OK with her going to Finn's yard if Samantha was there too! She wondered if there was any way she could sneak up to her bedroom to sort out her hat-flattened hair and nose reddened by the wind. Then she sighed. Finn never seemed to notice what she looked like, so

what was the point? Her jods and old fleece would have to do.

★

Alice chatted to Samantha as they travelled over to Rookham Manor, Finn's family home. It was a beautiful old building surrounded by parkland but all in need of renovation. Finn had explained to Alice last year that the house was held in some sort of trust, but the yard belonged to Sasha. Alice knew that Sasha was constantly worrying about the upkeep of both the yard and the horses and that money was tight. At least the stables damaged in the fire last summer were starting to be repaired. The fire had been started deliberately by Sasha's ex-boyfriend, Marcus, and it had taken a long time to get the money for repairs from the insurance company.

Finn, Angus and Sasha were in the yard and waved as Samantha's car pulled up. When

Samantha got out, Alice noticed Angus gave her a friendly hug. Alice remembered how he'd been at the party, so dismissive of the showing world, but Samantha was kind-hearted and loved horses, and had probably charmed him as she did everyone.

If Finn was surprised to see Alice with Samantha, he didn't show it.

"Do you want to meet the new pony?" he asked, and Alice nodded.

"You did say you wanted me to…" she stumbled, wondering if it was OK to turn up, but Finn just smiled at her and all her worries melted away.

Finn led the way to the part of the yard that had remained untouched by the fire. The horses were temporarily in internal stables in a rather decrepit old barn. Angus and Samantha followed a few steps behind.

"She's very wary of strangers," Finn said quietly to Alice.

A PONY called SECRET

There was a rustle from the stable and Alice saw a white flash, like catching a glimpse of a ghost. Finn turned on the lights and there at the back was the most beautiful mare, silvery grey with a long white mane and a delicate face. She was taller than Secret, perhaps nearer to fifteen hands, but much finer in build. Quietly letting himself into the stable, Finn spent a few minutes just talking to the little mare. Her ears were pinned back, her eyes rolling.

"This is Ella," Finn said softly.

"Remember what I said," Angus said in a gentle voice, edging into the stable. "Slowly, slowly. Let her know what you're doing. Neck first. Breathe in, breathe out, relax."

"What do you mean?" Alice whispered.

"If Finn is relaxed, it relaxes Ella," Angus replied. "We start with where Ella is happy to be touched, and then we work out from there."

Alice held her breath, watching as Finn stroked Ella on her neck using the flat of his hand, long strokes from the top of her mane downwards. Gradually her ears relaxed.

Then, as Finn gently pulled back her rug, Alice gave a cry of horror as she noticed the wound on Ella's shoulder. There were deep gouges, like a wild animal had clawed her. Although the flesh was clean and healed, the shoulder was almost concave, scooped out.

At the sound of Alice's voice, Ella flattened her ears again, backing into the corner, wildly snaking her head, and narrowly missing Finn as she lunged at him with bared teeth.

"Sorry," Alice whispered, mortified that she'd scared the pony, and Finn gave her a sympathetic look.

"It's OK," he said in the same low voice as his dad. "It's hard not to be shocked."

"What happened?"

Finn's eyes flashed. "We *think* her brand was carved out, to stop her being traced back to her owners," he said. "I'd guess she's a purebred Spanish horse. She's certainly got the looks. Removing the brand is probably not the worse thing that happened to her, which is why her behaviour is like this."

"When I came across her the wound was becoming infected," Angus explained. "She was found wandering around at the back of a tapas bar; she must have been dumped nearby. Alejandro, the bar owner, and his daughter tried to care for her – but they needed help. So I stepped in. I wanted to stay but when I heard about the fire I came home. So as soon as Finn and I could go back to get her, we did."

"Why would someone abandon her?" Alice asked quietly.

Finn sighed. "Who knows."

"She was lucky she'd been left where she was," Angus said. "She recovered quickly … physically at least."

"We also think she's been hit, so she has learnt to protect herself." Finn rolled up his sleeves and he showed Alice a display of bruises on his arms. You could see the teeth marks clearly.

At that moment Robin, Sasha's kindly grey horse, stuck his head over his stable door, and gave a friendly whicker. Ella gave a furious squeal and spun round, snapping the air with her teeth. Robin retreated with a startled look, as Sasha crossed over and gave him a cuddle.

"That's why the stable next to hers is empty," she explained. "She hasn't bonded with any of our horses."

"And how long will it take to train her?" Alice asked.

Finn looked at her. "Train her to do what?" he replied.

"OK, well, get her ... so she's not like this." Alice didn't know how to put her thoughts into words.

"I'm hoping by spring she'll be easier to handle," Angus said. "She's already come so far. She'd flinch every time we handled her at first, probably used to getting hit, or whipped. Her fear came out as aggression, and although it's better now she's still in defence mode."

"Why don't you put her out in the field so she can be free?" Alice asked.

Finn frowned. "She's terrified of being outside. We did try, but she just galloped around in a panic until we managed to get her back in. And, as you know, the fields here aren't exactly little pony paddocks."

Finn and Sasha's ponies roamed as a herd around

the parkland surrounding Rookham Manor. The set-up was very different to Alice's home, where the land was neatly fenced off into small paddocks.

Alice felt a pang in her stomach. Poor Ella, unable to enjoy the freedom of the land outside, to feel a breeze in her mane and the grass beneath her hooves.

"Why is she called Ella?" she asked as the mare turned her back to them.

Finn glanced at Alice. "Shortened from Rafaella. Alejandro's daughter. She looked after Ella while we waited to come back out. She couldn't do much, but she gave her water and hay every day. She was nice."

Alice felt a bubble of jealousy rise up and she quickly tried to suppress it, but she felt like all the air had been taken out of her, imagining Finn in the Spanish sunshine, bonding with Rafaella and rescuing her namesake.

"It's a lovely name," she said instead and Finn gave her a half-smile. Why did he always look like he knew what she was thinking?

TOP SECRET

Chapter 6

Angus invited them into the house for a hot drink. Samantha walked ahead with Finn, chatting about her plans for Archie, and Alice fell into step with Angus.

"Finn said you were competing tomorrow at the equestrian centre," Angus said, smiling. "I've been looking forward to meeting the famous Secret!"

A PONY called SECRET

Alice nodded, and started to tell Angus a bit more about her recent jumping sessions at home. He was very easy to talk to.

"It'll be fine, if he doesn't take off," she said. "He just locks on to the jumps, and I can't stop him. The actual jumping is no problem."

"I'll watch him tomorrow," Angus said in a kind voice, "and I'll be in a better position to advise. I hope you can come to our jumping lessons."

"We'll be there," Alice replied. Even though her mum was against it, she knew she had to do what was right for her and Secret.

Inside the house, Alice sat on the kitchen sofa with Lima, Finn's lurcher, snuggled into her. Finn perched on the sofa armrest next to her, and Alice could almost feel her leg burning from him being so close. They were just starting to discuss the show the next day when there was a shout from the yard. It was Sasha.

"Dad, Finn! It's Ella!" Her voice was shrill, urgent.

Jumping up, Angus raced to the door, as did Finn. Samantha gave Alice a worried look and they both got up to follow.

They were met with the sight of Sasha desperately hanging on to Robin, while Ella wheeled around and around. Her stable door lay on the floor, smashed to pieces.

"I was just leading Robin through," Sasha said tearfully. "Something must have spooked Ella and she went for him, breaking right through the door."

"OK, OK," Angus said, his voice calm and low. "She won't leave the barn."

Ella's head was aloft, her coat sweaty and her nostrils flared.

"Finn, you approach, I'll move the ponies," Angus continued, and Alice realised that two

ponies would now have to share a stable if Ella were to have an empty stable next to her.

Putting a head collar on Jill, one of the friendly Dales ponies, Angus put her in the same stable as Jack, her brother.

Finn walked up to Ella, quietly approaching her from the side. She rolled her eyes but didn't move as Finn laid a hand on her neck.

"Well done," Angus said, his voice soft. "Now, walk her into the stable."

Ella didn't even have a head collar on, but as Finn stayed by her side she started to move forward.

"She's so scared of being out of her stable that, even though she distrusts us, Finn is her safety net," Angus explained, as Ella shot into the waiting stable.

Everyone breathed a sigh of relief.

Finn and Angus surveyed the stable door. It was no more than firewood now.

Angus sighed deeply and turned to his son. "I don't think we've got a choice, Finn, I'm sorry. For her safety, and everyone else's, I think we'd better move her. It will only be for a few weeks."

Finn frowned. "It's not right for her," he said anxiously. "It's so … busy and commercial."

"What do you mean?" Alice blurted out. "Where's Ella going?"

Finn glanced at her. "You met Hannah?" he said, and Alice nodded. "Her dad offered us temporary livery at Hilltops equestrian centre, since Dad's going to be there a lot."

I bet Hannah had something to do with that! Alice thought, her mind whirring.

"It's not the best place," Finn continued. "But Dad's right. I don't think we have a choice now. This is the second stable door Ella has destroyed. She could really hurt herself."

Suddenly Alice had a brainwave.

A PONY called SECRET

"What about our place?" she blurted out. "We've got the two stables that Mum uses as an isolation unit. They've each got a small turnout paddock. Ella would be safe there..."

Angus gave her an incredulous look. "I'm not sure that would work, Alice, are you?"

But Finn looked as though he was seriously considering it. "Josephine's yard is lovely. And quiet."

"It's just our ponies, and a couple of client ponies until March," Alice continued. She hadn't a clue how she was going to ask her mum about this ... but she couldn't bear the thought of Ella at the equestrian centre! Not only did she want to see more of the mare, but she also hated the thought of Finn going over to Hannah's all the time.

Angus shook his head. "Thanks, Alice. But it's not a good idea," he said. "We'll take Ella to Hilltops, as discussed."

Alice's face fell. She really felt that Park Farm was the right place for Ella. She had to think of something!

★

Samantha dropped Alice home a little later. Alice went straight to the stables to help Fergus and Shelley with the evening routine, filling hay nets, skipping out beds and changing rugs. Then she decided to give Secret a good groom, ready for the showjumping. She'd already washed his mane and tail in the hot wash.

Fergus frowned as he saw her approach. "Alice!" he said in a cross voice, and Alice groaned. Fergus only ever used that voice when Secret had done something exceptionally naughty.

"Oh no, what's he done *now*?"

"I've just managed to get him back in; it took me twenty minutes to catch the little so-and-so. He's had the time of his life in the summer paddocks.

Go and see!"

Secret, always an escape artist, must have got out of his field somehow. Why did he always have to head for the muddiest fields?! The summer paddocks became boggy in winter, so Josephine let them rest, turning the ponies out in the paddocks next to the yard, which is exactly where Secret *had* been when she had left to go to Finn's.

Rounding the corner to Secret's stable, Alice felt her stomach drop. Someone had surely replaced her roan with a dark brown pony. Secret was plastered from head to toe in thick black mud, his mane hanging in solid clumps. Only his muzzle was visible.

"Secret!" Alice cried, and Secret, looking enormously pleased with himself, nodded his head up and down before kicking his rubber feed bucket out of the stable as if complaining his dinner was late.

"Oh, Fergus, please help me! I've got the showjumping tomorrow!"

Fergus tried to hide a smile. "I've turned the hot wash on ready for him." He sighed. "I swear he's half hippo!"

An hour later, after a lot of scrubbing and nearly a whole bottle of shampoo, Secret was once again red, drying off under the heat of the lamps, clad in two thick fleece rugs and still looking very pleased with himself. Alice looked down at her coat and jods, now plastered with mud, thinking it was probably a good thing she hadn't smartened up before going over to Finn's.

"You are a very naughty pony," she said affectionately, giving his fluffy coat a pat.

Fergus came back, looking exasperated.

"I've just checked the gates. The good news is he hasn't worked out how to undo the special latches," he said. "The bad news, or good,

A PONY called SECRET

depending on how you look at it, is he jumped to get to the good grass in the resting fields. At least you know he won't have any problems clearing the fences tomorrow!"

Chapter 7

The next day Secret was in good spirits. Tacking him up after they arrived at Hilltops, Alice huddled inside her thick fleece. As well as being cold, she felt *really* embarrassed about what had happened between her mum and Angus after the Flying Fillies display. She spotted Hannah sashaying across the lorry park. She was with Amy, one of the girls from the pony club party.

"Hey, Alice!" Amy smiled warmly, and Hannah gave a sort of half-smile that didn't quite reach her green eyes.

"Hi, Amy, hi Hannah," Alice said a little nervously, but then relaxed as Amy put a friendly hand on her arm.

"Are you OK?" she said in a kind voice. "Don't worry about what happened at the party. There's always some kind of drama; you should see what happens during camp week!"

Alice smiled gratefully. "Thanks."

"Yeah, but you have to admit, Amy, that was one of the more intriguing dramas we've seen!" Hannah said cattily.

Alice's face fell. She hated the thought of everyone talking about it.

"What class are you doing?" Hannah pressed. "Presumably the open, with me and the rest of the gang?"

"Um, no, the novice, the first one," Alice explained. "This is Secret's first proper jumping competition, although he's done a bit of showing."

"Oh, you'll be fine!" Hannah said breezily. "It's tiny. You'll be the oldest one in the class by miles; it's for the minis, really. I think some will be on the leading rein!"

Ouch. "Secret's young... He's only six," Alice started to say, but Hannah had turned away to check her phone.

"Good plan," Amy said, smiling at Alice. "A jumping competition has a different atmosphere to a show ring, doesn't it?"

Hannah turned back to Amy and Alice. "Finn's here!" She smiled. "Have you seen him?"

"No, we just got here."

Hannah tilted her head. "Never mind, I'm sure you'll see him later. He's been hanging out in our kitchen. It's soooo cold today!"

Alice gave a small smile, determined not to let Hannah get to her. Then she turned back to Secret. Alice desperately wanted to show Finn that she and Secret had improved, that they'd found the thing they both loved. And she needed to get their friendship back on track too. She was worried it would slip away again, like sand through her fingers.

★

The warm-up was busy. Secret jogged as Alice rode him round, his ears pricked and his breath a white plume in the icy air. Alice managed a trot and canter on both reins before taking a deep breath and waiting for a clear moment to jump. Aiming Secret towards the small cross pole, he broke into a sideways canter, pulling Alice towards the fence.

Secret overjumped by miles, leaving Alice clinging on as she struggled to right herself, feet searching for her lost stirrups.

"Well sat," a boy said, grinning and trotting calmly past. It was Jordan, and close behind him were a few more girls Alice recognised from New Year's Day. It seemed like the whole branch was here, and Alice wanted to make a good impression. Then, remembering the pressure she had put on herself over summer, Alice told herself not to be silly. She had stopped showing Secret as neither of them had enjoyed it … so she would just try to have fun.

Aiming Secret towards the jump again, Alice tried to keep her nerves steady. Ponies pick up on your emotions, so she had to think positive. After a few more jumps in the warm-up arena, Alice felt slightly calmer. They could do this!

There was still no sign of Finn as Alice sat shivering outside the indoor arena, waiting her turn. Her mum had thrown Secret's rug over his hind

quarters and had passed a hot chocolate to Alice, which she took a huge gulp of, before seeing Finn and his dad head into the seating area. And now the steward was waving her forward.

Entering the arena, with Secret spooking as the doors shut behind them with a bang, Alice suddenly felt as though the arena had tripled in size, the jumps ten metres high. All her earlier confidence evaporated. Picking up on her tension, Secret let out a high-pitched whinny. Alice pushed him into a wobbly trot as the bell rang and headed towards the first jump. Secret snorted as he found things to spook at: the arena mirrors, the spectators, the white banners advertising local businesses. His trot became slower and slower until he ground to a halt in front of the jump, and a groan went around the seating area.

Refusal at the very first! He'd never, *ever* refused before, but the atmosphere was so different here.

Alice knew it was her fault. She hadn't given Secret enough confidence and his desire to jump had been overridden by her hesitation. Giving him an apologetic pat, she was just about to turn him away when Secret took matters into his own hands and launched himself over. The groans from the crowd turned to a gasp as Alice tumbled off, landing neatly on her feet, still clutching Secret's reins. Her face was tomato red with shame. She really was making the biggest fool of herself! Dejected, she started to lead Secret out.

The steward gave her a kindly smile. "Finish your round if you like!"

Alice was confused. "But … I'm eliminated."

"It's only a fun show; confidence is more important than ribbons," the steward said. "Get back on and have a go, so you don't end on a bad note."

Thanking the steward, Alice clambered back

on Secret. She took a deep breath, determined to get it right this time, knowing what she had to do. Clucking at Secret and trotting a wide circle, she aimed him at the first jump, trying to think positively. Alice felt Secret hesitate for a second before she nudged him determinedly with her heels.

"Go on, boy!"

This time Alice was prepared. She clung on to a handful of red mane as Secret sailed over the small cross pole and landed in a smooth canter, heading for the next jump. Again, he cleared it by miles and started to relax, settling into a rhythmic canter. *He's enjoying himself*, Alice thought, *and so am I!* As Secret cleared the third, fourth and fifth jumps he no longer took off from several strides away. It was so smooth once he was in a rhythm. Forgetting her earlier mishap, Alice smiled in delight as Secret flew over the last jump. He was enjoying it so much it took Alice a couple of laps before she could pull up! She grinned, remembering how unmotivated she had been in the showing arena. Despite the refusal and the fall, she wanted to jump again, right away. Putting her arms round Secret she gave him a hug.

"Well done, boy. We made the right choice!"

The steward smiled at her as he let her back out. "Good for you. I told you it was worth carrying on!"

"Bravo!" A familiar voice welcomed Alice as she rode out of the arena. It was June Darby, standing next to her mum. "Well ridden, Alice. I can see your pony is a bit ... tricky, but what a super jumper!"

Alice glowed with pleasure, pleased she had impressed June, but slightly put out that she had called Secret tricky. At that moment he felt like the very best pony in the world!

"Have you met Angus, our new instructor?" June continued, falling in step with Secret. "He's here today."

Josephine looked up sharply.

"I know him," Alice mumbled.

"Ah, good. Then you'll know how wonderful he is," June said happily. "We're so lucky to have him signed up to teach. He's got experience from all over the world as well as being a fully qualified riding instructor. He'll bring the best out in you and your pony."

Alice hardly dared to look at her mum.

"We look forward to seeing you at our jumping lessons soon!" June said, smiling, before striding off to chat to some other pony club parents.

There was silence as Alice and her mum walked back to the horsebox, before her mum sighed.

"Look," she said, "you know it's not what I wanted. But seeing you in there on Secret, how you recovered yourself and carried on, I think that jumping could well be your thing and I don't want to stop you. If you want to stay in this branch, then fine. But if I'm unhappy with *anything* that man does, I'm pulling you straight out, do you hear me?"

Alice nodded, swallowing her surprise, and smiled. "Thanks, Mum, that means a lot to me."

She quickly loaded Secret and slipped out of the horsebox. Then she jumped as Finn appeared.

"Well done," he said warmly. "Awesome comeback!"

That meant more to Alice than anything. She thought she might burst with happiness.

Then Finn grinned wickedly. "Did the chocolate help?" he said, pointing to Alice's nose.

Alice glanced in the lorry window. Her nose was covered in dried hot chocolate.

Glaring at Finn, she hurriedly wiped it away.

A PONY called SECRET

"It did actually," she retorted. "Don't you know it's what all the top showjumpers wear on their faces?"

Finn laughed, and for a moment they had their old relationship back. Then it was shattered.

"Right, I've got to go and find Dad," he said. "We need to check out this stable for Ella."

Alice felt her stomach drop. "So you're moving her?"

"Just for a bit," Finn said. "Dad's right, it's not suitable at home. We've got no choice." Then he looked up as a friendly voice carried across the yard.

"Hey, Finn!"

Hannah. Alice narrowed her eyes.

Hannah appeared beside them and threw a dazzling smile at Finn. "Hi, you!" she purred. "I've got ages until I jump, so I thought I'd show you around properly. Give you the full tour!"

Then she turned to Alice. "Have you *heard* about Finn's poor mare?" she said dramatically. "We're *so* honoured to have her here!"

"I met her yesterday, at Finn's yard," Alice said, noting with quiet satisfaction the look Hannah threw her. *Ha*, she thought. *One to me!*

Hannah gave her an insincere smile. "Well, I'm looking forward to seeing her all the time," she said. "When she's *stabled* here."

Chapter 8

Alice decided to talk to her mum about Ella on the way home from the jumping. Her mum was in a good mood, and following her encounter with Hannah, Alice was even more determined that Ella shouldn't go to the equestrian centre.

"Mum?" she asked in her sweetest voice.

"Mmmm, what is it you're after?" her mum replied, throwing her an amused glance.

"Finn has a problem … a pony problem," Alice blurted out. "Their Spanish pony needs recuperation and their temporary stables aren't suitable."

"OK … and?" Her mum turned to her, raising an eyebrow.

"I just thought, well, we've only got a few ponies in the yard at the moment and it's quiet, so I wondered if the pony, Ella, could come and stay with us, just for a little while? I mean, Finn has done a lot for you and for Samantha." Alice's words came rushing out now. "In fact, remember how Finn *saved* Archie from the fire? And mum, Ella is beautiful and she's had such a hard time and she's getting better every day but—"

"OK, enough Alice!" Her mum sighed. "I'll think about it. But not right now."

Alice sat back and crossed her fingers. She just hoped she had done enough!

★

The first pony club group lesson was just a few days later. There were four others in Alice's group, including Jordan and Sam. Two girls, who Alice didn't recognise, both gave her friendly smiles. Alice remembered Hannah's snide words about Alice jumping in the same class as the little kids, but June had explained that the groups were divided up according to age rather than ability. So everyone did the same activities, concentrating on jumping or flatwork or any of the other disciplines the pony club offered. Some were better riders than others, but all were capable in the saddle.

Angus was in the centre of the arena. He had the same still, observant posture as Finn, carefully watching the ponies as they walked and trotted around the arena. After the showjumping competition Alice had been excited about showing

Secret off, but he was getting stronger and more excitable as they went around, squealing every time they passed the brightly coloured poles. Alice was already growing warm just trying to keep him in check.

Angus called the riders into the centre of the school. "OK, everyone, we're going to concentrate on some gridwork," he said, looking at each of them in turn. "I want to see control without interference, establishing the basics. It's all very well being able to jump the biggest jumps, but we need to get the foundations right first."

As the lesson progressed, Alice grew more despondent. Everyone else was doing brilliantly, but Secret wasn't listening to her – he was over-jumping everything, crashing through the grids and then taking off to do a lap of the arena while Alice tried to pull him up. As soon as he locked eyes on a jump, he became uncontrollable

in his enthusiasm.

"He's keen," Angus remarked mildly. "But, Alice, you need to relax. And let's try a neck strap so you don't yank him in the mouth when he over-jumps."

Rummaging in his rucksack, Angus pulled out an old stirrup leather that he quickly fastened round Secret's neck.

"Hang on to that, or his mane, when you jump," Angus explained. "Let's lower the jumps."

This time, with Angus standing next to the grid of tiny cross poles, Alice made a huge effort to relax and use her seat to try to steady Secret into the jumps. Sitting up straight, she clung on to the neck strap as Secret jumped through the grid, making sure she didn't interfere with his mouth. This time, he jumped the cross poles in a neater, controlled fashion.

"Very nice," Angus remarked. "With a pony

like Secret, we have to establish the basics. Lots of groundwork to strengthen your relationship. But he makes a lovely shape over the jumps, and I think you two have a good future. I'll enjoy teaching you."

★

A few days later Alice was at Finn's yard. To her delight, Finn had invited her over to see Ella again, and Josephine was collecting her on the way back from judging a competition. Alice had just heard her mum's four-by-four pull up on the driveway.

Alice was sure Ella looked a little healthier. But her eyes, full of distrust, told a different story.

Finn seemed worried. "I'm concerned she's going to freak out when we move her, and we'll be back to square one again," he explained. "The equestrian centre is nice, but it's just not right for Ella."

Before Alice could say anything, Alice's mum appeared round the side of the barn, and instinctively Alice put her fingers to her lips, worried her mum might startle Ella. Frowning, her mum moved closer as Ella appeared at her stable door, ears back, head snaking up and down. "My goodness," Josephine whispered, as she caught sight of Ella's injured shoulder.

At the sound of her voice, Ella pricked her ears and turned back, stretching her head forward. Before Finn or Alice could warn Alice's mum about Ella's snapping, something amazing happened. Josephine's outstretched hand connected with Ella's delicate muzzle, letting the little mare blow on to her hands. In the half-light of the barn, Alice could just see Ella's silvery white whiskers tickling her mum's palm as her mum stood quietly, gazing at the mare. Then Ella retreated, and the moment was gone.

"Wow!" Finn exclaimed. "That's the first time she's chosen to go to someone new. She didn't even do that with Dad or me!"

Josephine looked pleased. "What a gorgeous pony," she said. "I presume this is the one from Spain?"

Finn nodded, and before Alice could stop herself, she repeated Ella's predicament, rushing to tell her mum how the equestrian centre wasn't a suitable place for Ella to be.

"No, I can see that," her mum said when she'd finished talking.

Alice decided to take the plunge.

"She needs somewhere peaceful, somewhere she can recover properly, with space and access to the outside. Oh, Mum, please can she come and stay at Park Farm? Just for a little while? Please? You *did* say you'd think about it…"

Alice crossed her fingers as she looked at her

mum. She was gazing at Ella, a faraway look in her eyes. "How long does she need a place for?"

"A month… Two at most," Finn said, a glimmer of hope appearing in his face. "Until the stables are finished. They're nearly done, but with the snow forecast…"

Josephine sighed. "Well, we'd better go and discuss it then."

★

Alice and Finn sat awkwardly next to one another as Josephine and Angus negotiated taking Ella to Park Farm.

Angus was questioning Josephine's routines and who would look after her.

"Oh, for goodness' sake," Josephine snapped. "My staff and I are all perfectly experienced."

Angus leaned back on his chair. "Well, she's Finn's project, so if it's what he thinks is best, I'll go along with it," he said, glancing at his son.

Finn looked thoughtful. "I can get the bus straight from school, have time with Ella, and then be back in time to help with the evening stables. I'll do my homework at lunchtime."

"And I'll drop you over when I can. There's another thing, though." Angus frowned. "I don't want Finn working on Ella alone; there would need to be someone with him. Not to help, just to be around in case anything happens."

"Well, I can hardly just lend you one of my grooms every time Finn's doing something with the mare," Josephine snapped.

Alice spotted her chance. "I'll help!" she blurted out. "I'm in the yard all the time when I'm not at school. I'll make sure I'm around."

Finn smiled. "That would be amazing," he said, and Alice glowed with pleasure.

After a long pause Josephine sighed. "OK, if Alice is happy with that. It's just for a few weeks."

Alice and Finn escaped to the kitchen while Angus and Josephine talked logistics.

"Phew!" Alice grinned. "It was tense in there!"

"You're telling me. If only they'd get on!" Finn replied. "I know my dad feels bad about what happened with Blue."

Alice frowned. "Do you think," she said slowly, "having Ella at our house might…" She paused, not knowing how to word what she was thinking. "Might … make them get along? If they have to, for Ella's sake?"

Finn raised an eyebrow. "If Ella can mend that rift, she'd be a miracle worker!"

★

A few days later, Alice had another pony club lesson to attend. This time Hannah was in her group.

Angus was talking to June, so the pony club members warmed up alone to start with, chatting away to each other. Hannah rode Barney, a big Skewbald pony, right next to Secret, who put his ears back. He hated being crowded.

"So I hear you're expecting a new arrival," she said, her voice low.

Alice nodded, moving Secret away from Hannah's pony. "Finn rides for my mum, so it makes sense," she said in what she hoped was a casual voice, not mentioning her role in the negotiations. Hannah glared at her, but Alice didn't mind. She felt happy – and that seemed to rub off on Secret too.

Secret jumped everything beautifully, earning lots of praise from Angus. Alice's confidence was high, so when Angus started to run through the selection process for the showjumping team – explaining how he expected good attendance at all the group lessons, and about the trials themselves when the team would be chosen, Alice made

her mind up. She *would* try out for the team. She smiled, leaning forward to pat Secret. Everything felt OK.

After the lesson Alice rugged Secret up for the short journey home. The equestrian centre was only on the other side of the downs to Alice's house.

Amy came over and gave Alice a friendly smile. "We always have a drink in the café after lessons. Want to join us?"

Alice grinned. She looked at her mum, who nodded.

"Just for a bit," she said. "Secret can have his hay net and I'll check my emails."

Alice followed Amy over to the café. Ordering a hot chocolate, they joined the other riders.

Then Alice felt her happy bubble burst as the door swung open and Hannah strode in looking pleased with herself. She flopped down on to the sofa.

"What's up?" Amy asked.

"Finn's agreed to help me with Barney!" Hannah said smugly. "I've got something very special in mind for my party, and Finn's the only one who can help me."

"Oh!" said Amy, looking surprised. "Well … that's good news!"

"I know!" Hannah purred. "Plus, I want to secure my place in the showjumping team and I know some one-to-one time will help." She glanced at Alice. "Isn't it *great*?"

"Oh, Hannah!" Lola giggled. "You're so in there!"

Alice suddenly felt really awkward and so, after gulping down her drink, she left the café, bumping straight into Finn, who put both his hands on her arms to steady her.

"Alice!" he grinned. "Secret looked amazing

out there today!"

Alice nodded and managed a small smile.

"So, Hannah said you're coming over here to help her with her pony," she said casually.

"Well, yeah." Finn shrugged. "I'm going to be around anyway, with Ella just down the road at your house. I'm always happy to help if someone needs it."

That's not what she's interested in! Alice felt like screaming but instead she smiled cheerfully. "Of course!" she said in a bright voice.

Finn lowered his voice. "It's really for Dad as well. Hannah's dad pulls strings in this branch and I know Dad wants to make this teaching job permanent. So I couldn't really say no."

Alice felt relieved. He was doing it to help his dad, not because he liked Hannah. But as the big lorry pulled out on to the road home she couldn't stop the ball of worry in her stomach unravelling.

It seemed like Alice and Hannah were not only competing for a place in the showjumping team, but also for Finn's attention…

Chapter 9

Alice wasn't sure what to expect as Angus drove a trailer up to Park Farm the next morning. Ella had been vetted, and Alice and her mum had prepared one of the isolation stables for her.

It was another bitterly cold day, the odd snowflake drifting down into the yard and settling on the frozen grass. The radio in the tack room had been talking about this being the coldest winter on record. Alice and her mum were both wearing several jumpers and thick woolly hats, and they were still freezing.

There was a squeal and the sound of stamping and kicking as the four-by-four came to a halt. The trailer rocked from side to side like a boat in a storm. By the sound of the hooves on metal, they needed to get Ella out, and fast. Finn pulled on a hard hat, looking grim.

"It's going to be safer if we can back the trailer into Ella's new paddock," he explained. "I don't want to risk leading her across the yard."

Josephine had an incredulous look on her face as the trailer reversed, as if she couldn't believe what she had agreed to. Normally when ponies were delivered to Park Farm, they stepped quietly and calmly out of shiny lorries!

As Angus eased down the back ramp a moment later, Finn spoke in a low and calm voice to the grey

mare. Ella was at the back of the box, which had been banked up with a thick straw bed to protect her during the journey. Her ears were flat against her head and she looked terrified. The other ponies in the yard looked on in interest, perhaps sensing Ella wasn't like the other ponies that came and went for schooling.

Ella took a step forward, snorting, before launching herself back on her hocks and clearing the ramp of the trailer in one leap. Alice could see why Finn had suggested they didn't lead her! After Ella had flown around the small turnout paddock a few times, Finn guided her into the stable by laying a soothing hand on her damp shoulder. Like a shot, Ella flew inside.

"Can we leave the stable door open?" Finn asked. "Then she can choose to wander outside, if she feels more confident."

Calm was restored. The other ponies carried on

eating, and Ella snorted from the safety of her new home.

"We appreciate you taking her in," Angus said to Josephine.

"I'm doing this for Finn," Josephine said coldly, heading back to the house.

"I'd give Ella a few days to settle here," Angus said to Finn, "then resume what we were doing. I think it's best you go back to basics: touch, establishing body space, that sort of thing. She's going to be defensive for a while, settling into yet another home."

"I wish we could tell her she's safe here," Alice said, thinking aloud, and Angus smiled.

"It would be much easier, if we could talk to them," he said warmly. "But by using our body language and voice tone, we *can* communicate with her. I have a feeling she had a good start in life: a nice home, good training. There's something

there underneath the surface."

Alice felt able to ask Angus things about Ella that she had been wondering for the past few days.

"Why did you rescue her? I mean, it must have taken loads of time and money…"

Angus smiled. "You're asking why, out of all the thousands of ponies that might need help, why rescue Ella?"

Alice nodded.

"Truthfully, she just got to me," Angus said. "Something in her eyes. We can feel so helpless when faced with cruelty to animals, and it's happening all over the world. But someone said to me once: you can't change the world, but for the animal you are rescuing you *are* their world."

He paused, the same faraway expression Alice saw on Finn sometimes.

"Lima, Finn's dog, was the same. There were thousands of street dogs in South America. Beaten,

abused, starving. I wish I could've saved them all."
His eyes narrowed at the memory. "Lima just had
something about him asking to be helped. I guess
Ella reminded me of him in a way. Asking for help
in her own way."

Wow, Alice thought. Once again, she was
conflicted, torn between loyalty to her mum and
her admiration for a man who would go to great
lengths to rescue a pony after seeing something in
her eyes.

A few minutes later, Angus left and Finn and
Alice stood outside Ella's stable.

"So, what now?" Alice asked.

"We leave her be for a day or two," Finn said, his
eyes fixed on Ella. "I'll just sit out here quietly for
a bit to let her know she's OK, that I'm still here."

"But it's freezing," Alice said with a frown,
hoping Finn would ask her to stay with him. He
didn't.

"I'll be fine." Finn zipped his coat right up to his chin and pulled on a thick pair of gloves.

Dragging her feet, Alice joined Fergus and Shelley in the main yard to finish the rest of the stables routine. Every time she passed Finn he was sitting on an upturned bucket watching Ella. Unlike the rest of the ponies who were resting peacefully, Ella looked as if she might flee at any moment. Suddenly Alice had an idea, and slipped off into the house, where her dad was working on his computer at the kitchen table. He smiled as she whirled around, boiling a kettle and rummaging in the cupboards for mugs and biscuits.

"Is that the new pony of Finn's, the grey?" he asked, and Alice nodded. "She doesn't seem like mum's other ponies?"

Alice's dad wasn't horsey in the least but it seemed even he'd noticed something different about Ella!

Alice nodded again. "You could say that," she said. "But she's in good hands." And grinning at her dad she gathered everything up before crossing back over the yard, balancing two mugs of tea and a packet of biscuits.

She smiled shyly as Finn looked up with a start. "Thought you could use this."

He grinned. "Thanks."

Alice perched on another bucket, warming her hands on the mug.

"Why was your dad so keen that we didn't get involved with her?" Alice asked.

"Well, he just wants Fergus to do her basic day-to-day care, and I'll do the rehab," Finn said. "He thinks it'll confuse her if lots of people get involved."

"Oh."

Alice was disappointed. She had hoped Finn might have trusted her to do some work with Ella

while he wasn't there.

Seeing her hurt expression, Finn smiled.

"But you'll help massively," he said, and Alice's heart leapt, "by just being here when I handle her. Little and often is best. We'll start by going back to basics like Dad said, and hopefully by the time she goes we'll have progressed outside, and maybe we can even try some exercises."

"Sounds great!"

Intrigued, Alice looked over at Secret, who was cheerfully trailing hay over his stable door. She wondered what he'd be like if he had fallen into the wrong hands. She shuddered, preferring not to think about it. Remembering what Angus had said about changing the world for one animal, Alice really hoped it would change for Ella.

Chapter 10

The next day Finn was back at the yard early to muck out Ella's box, and he had his mountain bike with him.

The door to Ella's stable was open, but judging by the lack of hoof prints or droppings on the frosty ground, Ella hadn't left its safety. She gave a snort as Finn quietly pushed a wheelbarrow in. Alice had noticed that he always wore a hard hat

when he was around Ella. This was unusual, given that Finn rarely wore a hat during his stunt work.

When Alice pointed this out, Finn gave a rueful grin. "She's already bitten me on the head, and it really hurt!"

Once the stable was mucked out Finn quietly slipped a head collar on Ella, who pinned her ears back. Finn slowly and gently unfastened her rug and rolled it back, and again Alice winced at the scarring across her shoulder. She held her breath as Finn placed a hand on the skin, where the hair was just starting to appear back, and held it there for a while, closing his eyes and talking to Ella in a low, quiet voice. Alice watched as the little mare visibly relaxed, her tension starting to drain away.

"What are you doing?" she whispered.

"Touch is a powerful thing," Finn explained quietly. "By putting my hand on her injured shoulder, and thinking to myself *'I know what you've been through'*, I think Ella feels it somehow."

Alice was fascinated. "Can I say hello to her?"

Taking her cue from Finn she quietly let herself into the enclosure, and approached Ella. Automatically she reached her hand out to Ella's nose, giving it a pat. That was how she greeted every pony she met. Immediately Ella's ears went back and, swinging her head, she snapped her teeth against Alice's hand. Alice only just managed to pull back in time.

"What did I do?"

"You went in all wrong, over-familiar," Finn said, raising an eyebrow at Alice. "Ponies actually hate having their noses fiddled with. Imagine an aunty ruffling your hair when you were little. It just irritates Ella, gets her cross."

Alice felt hurt. "But I do that to Secret all the time! I always pat his nose and wibble his lip around. He likes it…"

Finn gave a smile. "Secret's a good-natured pony. He's never had anything bad happen to him, unlike Ella. So, although you might be annoying, he loves you, so he puts up with it. Do you notice he often starts to play with your hand when you do it?"

Alice thought hard. "Well, yes, that's why I thought he liked it."

"He's asking you politely to stop it, unlike Ella who just snaps at you."

Alice slumped. "So how do you approach Ella?"

"Here, look." Finn put his hand on Ella's shoulder again, holding his hand out flat and giving Ella one firm stroke, before moving it away. "Horses have amazing vision," he said. "If you approach her quietly to the side, rather than going straight up to her face and getting in her space, she's more likely to invite you in than to go into defence mode."

★

When Alice went to see Secret a bit later she placed a hand on his shoulder, exactly like Finn had with Ella. She was pleasantly surprised when Secret seemed to relax under her touch, almost as if he was giving a sigh of relief. Alice smiled to herself. Having seen how Ella reacted to different body language, it made her think about how she should approach all ponies, even the friendliest ones like Secret.

★

Finn had offered to ride out with Alice, and she hoped he would notice how much more relaxed she and Secret seemed with each other as he rode Lachlan alongside her.

"My dad said he thought you were great together the other day," Finn said, and Alice blushed with pride.

"He's a brilliant instructor," she smiled.

"Yeah, I guess he is," Finn said. "I forget sometimes he's a qualified riding instructor, because, you know, he's my dad. I know he showjumped professionally for a bit before I came along. I think he'd like to have a permanent position with the pony club. Just as long as *I'm* not in the lessons!"

Alice grinned, thinking about her mum. They'd argued more than once when Josephine had taught her!

As they rode back into the yard, the ponies relaxed on loose reins, Alice was just summoning up the courage to ask Finn if he wanted to join her for a late breakfast when he glanced at his watch and gave Alice an apologetic look.

"I said I'd go over to the equestrian centre," he said. "Hannah will have Barney waiting for me."

Watching him cycle off, Alice couldn't ignore the sinking feeling in her stomach. Remembering

Finn's words about doing it for his dad, she tried to reason with herself but couldn't. Hannah would be waiting there: pretty, popular and determined to get closer to Finn.

★

Finn was over at Park Farm most days with Ella. Alice tried not to get in his way, and instead watched from the fence, taking it all in. Finn had been working on getting Ella used to contact again.

"Now I can start to groom her," he explained. "I can't wait to get her looking good again."

"Amazing!" Alice said, thrilled. "She'll be able to go outside soon, won't she?"

Finn shook his head. "That's just what Hannah suggested," he said and Alice's stomach dropped, imaging him and Hannah having cosy chats during their secret work with Barney. "That's my biggest hurdle," Finn continued, seemingly oblivious to Alice's frown. "It's OK getting her used to us here,

as this is where she feels safe. She'll go outside when she's ready."

Then before he could explain any further, Josephine came over.

"Finn, we need to talk about your mare," she said briskly.

"What about her?"

Josephine frowned. "Both Fergus and Shelley have been bitten while mucking Ella out, and I can't risk them getting badly hurt, or Ella getting injured. She needs specialist care."

Finn looked at her. "I'd like to come over before school and do it myself," he said flatly. "But with the other ponies, I just can't manage it."

Josephine gazed at the little mare. Ella was eying her warily, but stood calmly next to Finn. Josephine's expression softened, and she sighed.

"I'll deal with her in the mornings," she said. "Can you show me how best to approach her?"

Josephine had a lifetime's experience with ponies, but she still listened carefully to Finn as he explained the best way to open the stable door and approach Ella so as not to startle her, and how to put her at ease before mucking out.

Angus seemed pleased about Josephine helping when he collected Finn a little later. "That's what I'd hoped for," he said. "Not that I don't think you have brilliant grooms, but I'd like as few people as possible involved with Ella. And you've always been brilliant with tricky ponies, Josie."

Alice noticed that her mum completely ignored this compliment.

"I'd rather you don't comment on how I run my business, Angus," she said tightly. "I'll deal with Ella's care, Finn does the handling, and soon it will be spring and we can all get back to normal."

Chapter 11

A few mornings later, Alice was racing to catch the school bus when singing drifted over the yard on the still, frozen air. Stopping in her tracks, Alice headed over to Ella's stable. Inside her mum was singing softly to Ella as she stood close to her and Ella was nuzzling her mum's shoulder affectionately. Stunned, Alice turned back for the bus, only just catching it in time. She'd never seen her mum act like that with a pony other than Lachlan!

★

Her mum was back in business mode when Alice got home later that afternoon. She had only just gone over to say hello to Secret when her mum yelled at her to come into the office. As Alice quickly shut the stable door, Secret kicked it hard, annoyed at her disappearance. Hurrying into the office, Alice saw that her mum was busy filling in entry forms for the first shows of the spring.

"This will be Lachlan's final year in the ring." At the mention of her beloved Highland's name, her mum's voice softened, as she gazed up at a framed photo of the gelding at the most recent Olympia, his reserve championship sash proudly round his strong neck.

"I'll miss riding him at shows," Alice said

truthfully. Lachlan, after Secret, was her favourite pony.

"I was thinking I might even get on him again once he retires, hack around the lanes," her mum said, her eyes shining.

"Really?" Alice couldn't remember the last time she'd seen her mum on a horse.

"Seeing you on Secret recently has brought back lots of old memories," her mum replied with a smile. "I miss riding."

Their conversation was interrupted by a yell from Fergus. "SECRET!"

Alice's mum looked at Alice resignedly. "You'd better go and sort him out."

Outside, Alice was met by an exasperated Fergus, who held the special clip for Secret's stable door in his hand.

"Ooops!" Alice had been so distracted by her mum calling that she'd forgotten to put Secret's clip back on the door bolt. He was gleefully heading from stable to stable, greeting each of his friends.

"Go and get him!" Fergus said crossly. "Honestly, he's nothing but trouble!"

Racing over to the tack room to grab Secret's head collar and a scoop of feed, it took Alice a few seconds to realise that Secret was trotting purposefully across the yard and heading straight for Ella.

"Secret, no!"

Racing after him, Alice rattled the feed scoop, desperately trying to get his attention, but the little red gelding totally ignored her.

Hearing the commotion, Ella appeared at the door of her stable as Secret came to a stop outside the gate to her enclosure. She squealed furiously, throwing her head up and down. Secret, undeterred, whickered back. Then Alice's mouth fell open in disbelief as Ella slowly placed one

hoof outside her stable, before snatching it back in. Her ears were back in anger, but her eyes were fixed curiously on Secret. Then she took another step, and this time the hoof stayed outside. She took another step forward, then another, creeping slowly out until her whole body was outside the stable. For a second her white mane lifted in the breeze, shining in the winter sun, as she paused to sniff the air. Then she flew towards Secret, teeth bared.

Leaping forward, Alice grabbed Secret's mane, trying to pull him away. But Secret stayed where he was, lowering his head and breathing out. The ponies' muzzles touched briefly before Ella gave a squeal, striking out with a foreleg. This didn't put Secret off and once again their muzzles connected, sniffing, nostrils flared. Ella stayed next to Secret, the white pony next to red.

"What's going on?"

Alice jumped as Finn appeared behind her.

"I'm so sorry…" she started to say, thinking Finn would be furious.

"Did Secret get out?" Finn sounded anxious. "We should catch him before Ella does some damage to him."

Alice looked at the ponies again. They were starting to groom each other over the fence, and Ella's ears were forward, her eyes soft.

"You said she hadn't bonded with any of your ponies, right?" said Alice. Finn nodded. "So … Secret is the first pony Ella's allowed near her since she arrived in England. Isn't this a good thing?"

A smile crossed Finn's face. "I didn't want to risk any of your ponies getting hurt, but if Ella trusts another pony, that will really help her confidence," he said. "Horses are herd animals; they're not meant to live alone."

"What about moving Secret in next door?"

Alice turned round, startled. She hadn't realised her mum had been quietly observing.

"I've felt sorry for poor Ella out here alone. Secret's a brilliant companion," Josephine added.

Alice looked at her mum in surprise. It was one thing singing to Ella and taking over her care, but moving ponies around was a big deal for her. She realised that her mum had grown fond of Ella.

"Great," Finn enthused. "If that's OK."

And so Alice and Finn made up a bed next door to Ella. Alice smiled as Secret bustled into his huge stable. The isolation stables were the biggest on the yard and Secret looked as though he was in heaven, taking a mouthful of his hay net before going to check on Ella, who looked the most relaxed Alice had seen her. The evening had closed in, a blanket of stars overhead. It was going to be another freezing night.

"Oh no, I've missed my bus," Finn said, looking

at his watch and frowning. "I'll have to get Sash to collect me."

Pulling his phone out of his pocket, he texted his sister. Alice was secretly pleased to have a bit more of Finn's time, and even more pleased he wasn't heading over to Hannah's house! However, twenty minutes later, it was Angus who pulled up in the old Landrover.

"Hello, Alice!" Angus said warmly and she smiled in response.

Then Angus looked up as Josephine came out of the house, and the atmosphere changed. The two grown-ups nodded to each other briskly.

"It's great that Secret is next to Ella," Angus said.

Alice blushed. "Yeah. Secret sort of escaped and I couldn't catch him," she explained. "And then he came over to see Ella."

"Fantastic," Angus said. "That should really help. A mini herd!" Then he added, "Alice, I've

got a bit of time this week, if you fancy a private session. Just so you're ready for the next pony club lesson? It would be good to have it over at Hilltops so Secret's in a new environment. Call it a thank-you, for Secret's help with Ella!"

Alice didn't even pause. "Yes please!" she said enthusiastically, and then she glanced at her mum, who had a face like thunder.

Chapter 12

It snowed on and off for the next couple of days, flakes drifting down and settling on the frozen ground, before everything seemed to stop, and the temperature plunged even further. The yard thermometer had recorded minus thirteen degrees overnight, the coldest it had ever been.

When Alice got back from school one afternoon she saw Fergus peering up at the sky as he

stamped his feet to keep them warm. "It's too cold to snow properly," he said. "Once it warms up a few degrees, then we'll be in big trouble."

"What about the ponies?" Alice said in a worried voice, and Fergus grinned.

"Al, I'm from the Highlands," he said with a chuckle. "Believe me, anything we get down here will be nothing compared to up there in winter. Will it, boy? Do you remember the snow that fell when you were just a foal?" He gave Lachlan, who had been listening with interest, a friendly scratch.

Alice smiled at Lachlan and Fergus. She knew the big Highland meant a lot to the groom. Fergus's late dad, a big name in the Highland showing world, had bred Lachlan. She loved listening to Fergus talk about Lachlan's first year up in Scotland, and tell the story of how her mum had fallen in love with him from a photograph.

"I'll tell you what, though," Fergus lowered his voice, "your mum seems to have fallen in love with Ella. I actually heard her *singing* to her the other morning!"

Alice smiled. "Don't tell her you heard that!" But it was true; her mum seemed besotted with the little mare.

"By the way, Finn's over; he's in with Ella." Fergus gestured towards the isolation stables and Alice felt her heart flip. He was early. Ashamed that her first thought was that she hadn't had time to change out of her dreaded school uniform, she raced round to Secret and Ella's stables, before slowing down as Finn put a finger to his lips. Secret was standing next to the adjoining fence in his small turnout paddock, and next to him, one leg resting contentedly, was Ella. She was outside!

"She was like this when I got here," Finn explained.

"That's amazing!" Alice whispered. "Well done, Ella!"

"It's thanks to Secret really, and you," Finn smiled. "What do you say to us trying some new things this weekend? Are you about?"

"There's a pony club lesson on Saturday morning, but I'm free afterwards. What do you have in mind?" Alice said, intrigued. Finn had said 'us', she noted with pleasure.

"I thought we could take her out in hand, with Secret," Finn explained. "Just try a short loop away from her stable at first, so she knows her safe place is nearby."

"Go on?" Alice said.

"If Ella's confident about going out, we can take them round the tracks, find some tiny logs to step over, that sort of thing," Finn continued. "The aim is to get Ella to think about something else. It will really help build up her confidence."

"And you think Secret will help?" Alice asked, looking at her pony who was gazing adoringly at Ella.

"Absolutely," Finn explained. "Once she's confident going with Secret, we can even try her on her own."

"Can't wait!" Alice enthused, and it was true. She had never been so excited about *not* riding Secret before!

"Right, I'm off to Hannah's now," Finn said.

Alice felt her heart sink. She had hoped she'd have some more time with Finn. Then she saw him looking at her closely.

"You just made a weird face, Alice. What's up?"

"Nothing!" Alice blushed. "What do you actually do there, anyway?"

"I'm not meant to say," Finn said after a pause. "We're working on something for her party."

Alice's imagination went into overdrive. What

was Hannah getting Finn to help her with?

"Hannah always asks after you, you know," Finn continued.

Does she now? Alice thought bitterly. Maybe she had the wrong idea about Hannah… Finn seemed to like her, didn't he? Maybe *Alice* was the problem!

★

"You only need to ask if you want *me* to give you a one-on-one jumping lesson." Her mum frowned as she drove Alice and Secret over to the equestrian centre later in the week. "I don't have Angus's qualifications but I do know a bit. And I know you and Secret. Angus doesn't…"

The statement hung in the air.

"I know, Mum, and we love our flatwork lessons with you," Alice said slightly guiltily. "But it is useful to have different opinions and group lessons, as well."

"Well, I can't argue with that, and Angus has impressed the pony club," Alice's mum said, drumming her fingers on the steering wheel. "But remember what I said, if I'm unhappy about anything he suggests…"

Alice nodded. For all his good work recently, her mum still couldn't forget that Angus' advice had led to Blue's accident.

Alice gazed down at her carefully chosen outfit. Normally when she schooled she rode in tatty jogging bottoms and old fleeces full of holes. But Alice wanted to look grown up and professional and like a budding showjumper. She had used the last of her Christmas money to buy a pair of breeches from the local saddlery. She still wasn't quite sure about them, but she'd been talked into them by the girls in the shop – they had bright checks with a silver flash down the side. Alice was also wearing a red shiny jacket covered in diamante

that had been reduced in the sale. She hoped she looked OK, or better than OK! She didn't feel like herself at all.

Finn was in the school with Hannah and her pony when Alice arrived. Peeking her head round the door, Alice watched for a moment, unseen. Finn seemed to be showing Hannah how to draw Barney into her by using body language. Alice bristled as Hannah smiled up at him, not looking at Barney. She couldn't look any less interested in her pony, but Finn seemed oblivious. Alice recognised the faraway look he had when he got really absorbed with his work. Then Hannah spotted her and a sly grin spread across her pretty face.

"Alice, how *are* you?" she said, waving. "Come in!"

Sidling in, Alice wished she had stuck to her normal outfit. Hannah looked so pretty and understated in jeans and cowboy boots and a cropped Puffa jacket.

Finn gave a start as he looked at Alice, and a confused expression crossed his face.

"What?" Alice tugged self-consciously at her coat, trying to pull it down over the breeches. Outside they seemed even brighter.

"You look ... um, different." Finn was still staring at her sparkly coat with a strange look on his face.

Alice felt a rush of anger. "And? What's wrong with different? It's OK for you, isn't it, Finn Cutler? Always so cool. Well, I LIKE my new clothes, so there!"

Suddenly aware of Hannah smirking, Alice flushed, the adrenalin from her outburst fizzing through her.

Finn looked mortified. "That's not what I meant..."

But Hannah had now burst into peals of laughter

and both Finn and Alice turned to her.

"Oooh," Hannah said, opening her green eyes very wide. "You and your mum certainly share a temper, don't you?"

Alice gaped at Hannah, the blood rushing to her ears. She couldn't think of a reply.

Realising Barney had wandered over to the far end of the school, Hannah headed off to catch him, but not before laying a hand on Finn's arm.

"Thanks for another great lesson," she said, smiling up at him. "I feel our connection is just getting *so* much deeper, you know?"

Your connection with Barney or your connection with Finn? Alice thought sourly, noticing that Hannah was just the right height to peer cutely up at Finn. Unlike Alice, who would be taller than him if she ever bothered to wear boots with heels. How could Finn not realise what was so obvious? And what *were* they working on?

Finn turned to Alice. "I'm so sorry, Alice," he said, looking right at her. "That came out all wrong. Your new clothes are nice; I was just surprised. They're quite, um, shiny, and I've never seen you wear anything like that. The truth is…" He held her gaze, and Alice dropped it first. "The truth is I think you always look great, really great. Whatever you're wearing."

Alice opened her mouth to argue back when the enormity of what Finn had just said hit her. That was the first thing he had ever said that hinted that possibly, just possibly, he liked her. She felt herself blush ever harder, cursing her pale skin, which reddened easily.

"Yes, well." She stuck her nose in the air, wishing that Hannah had overheard *that* bit of the conversation! "*I* like the shininess, and I don't care what you think about my clothes." And that, she realised, was the truth.

Finn smiled, his dark eyes twinkling. "Good for you."

Feeling newly confident, Alice strode back to Secret and tacked him up, swinging herself up into the saddle and heading back to join Angus. She was pleased she had stood up for herself, and had butterflies over Finn's compliment. Clothes didn't matter one bit. She had something far more important to think about. Her relationship with Secret.

Chapter 13

Angus stood in the centre of the arena watching Alice and Secret canter a circle. Secret's natural impulsion and self-carriage meant Alice really didn't have to do a huge amount to look impressive on the flat. When Secret was going forward he looked amazing.

"Lovely, Alice," Angus said. "Now pop that cross pole, and let's see what we need to do."

A PONY called SECRET

Alice's mouth went dry as she turned Secret towards the jump. It wasn't that she didn't love the jumping; it's just that she knew that it could go either way – Secret could either jump nicely, or launch himself over. Clinging on to the neck strap as Angus had instructed her, Alice felt Secret start to bounce sideways. It was going to be one of *those* days. She tried to check him, to get him back under her control, but Secret was already bounding towards the jump and cleared it by miles.

Unseated, one stirrup lost, it was all Alice could do to stay on as she circled the arena. They jumped a couple more times in much the same fashion, before Angus put his hand up to stop them. Secret was bright-eyed and his ears were pricked as he nuzzled Angus's shoulder. Alice bit her lip. She would never make the showjumping team if she couldn't control Secret.

As if reading her thoughts, Angus smiled. "OK," he said in a kind voice. "Secret's a talented pony and, Alice, you are a lovely rider. But I think what's happening is that you're anxious about each jump session, and Secret picks up on that. Do you know what would help?"

Alice shook her head.

"Not jumping at all," Angus said. "Secret needs to relax, to focus. What I'd suggest is just hacking, finding little things to pop over on your rides, and NO jumping in the school. Instead, I want you to put some poles down: walk, trot and then, when you're confident, canter over them. Play around with them with Secret loose in the school and you on the ground. Go out on your farm, if you feel up to it. If you focus on your groundwork and flatwork, then the jumping falls into place. Here, look."

Angus quickly dismantled the cross pole, laying

the poles around the arena. Then Alice rode over them at walk. At first, Secret bounded sideways, leaping the poles but, encouraged by Angus, Alice concentrated on her seat and her breathing. After a few minutes, Secret started to settle down and walked over the poles. By the end of their lesson she had managed a calm and controlled canter on both reins, with no leaping about. It felt brilliant – harmonious and relaxed.

Angus praised Secret as the little gelding rested his muzzle on his shoulder. "And that's what you need to do, Alice," he said. "We'll have jumping lessons with pony club, but at home just ride him. If you must school him, do it on the flat around the jumps, so he doesn't get excited every time he sees the coloured poles. With a pony like Secret it's important you don't let him burn out."

Alice nodded. It made sense. She noticed her mum was sitting on the mounting block watching.

"Well done, Alice, and well done, Secret," Josephine said, strolling towards the pair. "He reminds me of Blue." Her voice stumbled on her pony's name. "I hardly jumped Blue at home either, because of how he could be."

Her expression was thoughtful, reflective even. As if she was thinking about happier days with Master Blue.

★

The pony club group lesson, a few days later, was less successful.

"OK, Alice, your turn!" Angus called, and Alice's stomach somersaulted as she took a deep breath. Snatching at his bit, Secret cantered on the spot before plunging down the line of jumps, and then he circled the arena at such speed that he almost hit Jordan's pony, who put his ears back and spooked to the side.

"Hey!" Jordan steadied his pony, giving him a

pat as Alice apologised.

Humiliated, Alice stood aside for a bit, trying to calm Secret down. To make matters worse, Hannah, the best rider in the group, jumped beautifully, her skewbald pony calm and relaxed as he popped neatly through the grids.

"Good boy," Hannah said loudly as she patted her pony. "You're not worried about any silliness, are you?"

This comment was clearly aimed at Alice and Secret. Alice reddened, and Secret chose that exact moment to whinny loudly and dance on the spot, keen to get going again.

Finn came over to the arena fence. He'd been watching from up in the gallery.

Alice made a face. "I can't control him," she said miserably.

Finn leaned over the fence. "Of course you can," he said firmly. "You need to relax!"

After that things did improve a bit. Angus let Alice jump right at the end once the others had finished and Secret had calmed down. As they jumped through the grid, taking off perfectly, landing and cantering away in one smooth movement, Alice started to once again believe that they had a chance at making the team.

Alice hoped to have a proper chat with Finn after the lesson, but Hannah reached Finn first.

"Any chance you can stay a bit?" Hannah said to Finn in a pleading voice, totally ignoring Alice. "I really want to practise a bit more."

Finn shrugged. "OK," he answered to Alice's disappointment.

Hannah gave Alice a triumphant smile. Then her tone changed.

"I can't wait for my party now," she said. "Can you?" She coyly dropped her eyes, fluttering her long lashes. "With you by my side it's going

to be amazing."

Finn looked slightly bemused. Not for the first time Alice wondered if he was so wrapped up in his ponies that he didn't even notice when girls flirted with him... But what did Hannah mean? Was Finn going *with* her to the party?

"Yeah, it should be good," he said vaguely. "Alice, you're coming, aren't you?"

Hannah glared at Alice, before her expression changed. Giving Alice a huge smile, she placed a hand on her arm. "Of course Alice is coming!" she cried, tilting her head to one side.

"Well," Alice cleared her throat, feeling awkward. "You mentioned it a little while ago, but I didn't get an invitation."

"Oh! Well, do come, won't you? You must!" Hannah said in the sweetest voice, but her eyes told a different story.

Chapter 14

Alice thought about the party a lot over the next few days. She didn't have anything to wear and Hannah had told everyone they had to go all out on their Winter Wonderland themed outfits. Suddenly Alice had a great idea. Samantha had a dressmaker friend who helped out with the Flying Fillies costumes. Maybe she could make something for Alice? If she was going to go to the party, then

she wanted to look her best. And it *would* be nice to dress up for once!

At least Alice had the chance to spend some time with Finn over the weekend. They were going to walk Ella out in hand, with Alice leading Secret. Finn explained that they would start with a short walk away from the yard in a petal shape, so that Ella would know the safety of her box was near. There were plenty of walkways in between the paddocks, making short routes around the farm, even in winter.

As they were heading out of the yard, Alice's mum came out to say hello to Ella. Alice noticed the little mare crane her neck to greet her, ears pricked and eyes soft.

"What are you doing?" she asked, sounding interested, and Finn briefly explained.

"What a good girl." Josephine gave Ella's neck a gentle stroke. "Have fun!"

Alice held her breath as she and Secret walked on, with Ella and Finn almost level with them. Secret was excited to be going out in the direction of the summer paddocks, where he enjoyed cantering around with his friends.

"No, Secret." Alice gave his lead rope a tug as he jogged, trying to get ahead of her. Glancing at Finn, she noticed the long rein was almost slack in his hand, as Ella walked to his shoulder.

"Secret still tows you to the field?" Finn said with a smile. "When it snows you can put skis on."

Alice glared at him. "Oh, funny."

"You need to establish your body space," Finn said. "He knows he can completely invade your space and that's why he literally walks all over you."

Alice grimaced. "How? He's so strong."

"Here, stop a minute," Finn said. "You need to get your adrenalin levels down. Stand in front of

him, look at him, but keep your hands down. If he steps into your space, make him go back. Not by slapping him or anything like that, just make a sound or step towards him. Just relax and breath out. It will all help to bring Secret down. You're getting wound up every time you lead him out."

"I thought we were here for Ella, not Secret," Alice replied miserably.

Finn grinned. "I think it's good for all of us!"

As they headed back down the track towards the yard, their breath like clouds in the freezing air, Alice realised Finn was right. By establishing her body language with Secret, he was actually walking beside her rather than dragging her along.

"It's what I've been doing with Hannah," Finn said out of the blue. "Working on body language and stuff. She's trying out for the showjumping team. Are you going to try? Dad thinks you should."

Hannah again. Alice frowned. She always seemed to get mentioned.

"Hopefully," she said shortly.

Finn give her a strange look. "So, I think that's enough for today," he said. "It's a really big step for Ella to just walk out this far."

"Mum will be proud," Alice replied. "She likes her."

"I've noticed. Ella seems to make her happy."

Alice nodded. "You should see her with Ella in the mornings. Singing to her, taking ages doing her stable. And she's always asking about what you're doing next with her. I've only ever seen her like that with Lachlan."

"She's got something special about her," Finn said, placing a hand on Ella's white mane. "Her movement is out of this world; she would have made a good dressage pony. You can tell someone loved her."

Alice imagined Ella in her previous life. Had she belonged to a girl, just like Alice, who adored and doted on her? Had she been a champion, or just someone's best friend?

★

Alice and Finn took Ella and Secret out for longer the next day, completing a whole loop of the tracks between the paddocks. Encouraged by Finn, Alice had unclipped Secret's lead rope for a bit. She'd expected him to just eat, or run away, but he'd trotted alongside Ella, following Alice as she zigzagged between branches and skipped over a couple of fallen logs.

Alice's cheeks were flushed with cold and happiness as they reached the top track. When Alice had been younger she and Honey used to ride the same loop, making jumps out of twigs and small branches she found, and she felt like she was eight years old again, out playing with her pony.

"This is so much fun!" she enthused, leaping over a small log herself, and then blushing as Finn grinned at her.

"You make me laugh!" he said, his voice warm, and Alice felt the closest they'd been in a long while. She smiled back at him, and for just a few seconds they gazed at each other before Finn moved in a step closer, and Alice felt her heart thud.

Then Finn's phone beeped and he pulled it out. Typing something in reply, a smile spread across his face. Alice felt as though she had been punched in the stomach, the happiness of the previous half hour gone, the moment shattered. It was Hannah; it had to be. Alice might make him laugh, pretending to be a pony, but he never smiled like that with her.

Chapter 15

The showjumping team was now the main topic of conversation between the riders – with everyone wondering who would make the final four. Angus's lessons meant all the riders had a renewed enthusiasm for jumping, and with the prospect of intensive training and area competitions, everyone wanted to make the team. Alice even found herself daydreaming about wearing the blue jacket with

Hilltops Showjumping Team emblazoned on the back!

Her dad took her to the next lesson as her mum was away, and Alice was looking forward to showing him how much she and Secret had progressed.

As Alice rode into the arena she felt confident, but although the lesson started well it soon began to unravel. Secret was bright and alert as he snorted and spooked at the jumps. As he grew more flighty, her confidence faded.

"Sit up!" Angus called as they flew round the corner to the last fence on the course: a simple spread with a brightly coloured filler. Feeling Secret look at the jump, Alice tensed, pulling back on the reins without realising.

"Neck strap!" Angus called but it was too late.

Taking off from two strides away, Secret cleared the small jump like it was the puissance wall,

his back feet catching the poles and sending the whole jump tumbling down. The wing crashed to the ground and Alice was unseated. The soft sand came up to meet her as she rolled on to her side, with Secret's hooves missing her head by millimetres. Then, as if he realised Alice was no longer on board, he slowed, and turning a circle came back to her, eyes bright, reins trailing as he nudged her.

Alice's dad rushed into the arena looking panicked, but Hannah rolled her eyes. "She's fine," she called in a bored voice as Angus knelt down next to Alice's dad.

Tears pricked Alice's eyes. It was no good; they weren't ready for this, Alice thought miserably.

Her dad put an arm round her shoulder. "You and your ponies!" he said in a kind voice, and Alice started to cry.

"Hey," Angus said gently. "Don't be like this!

You're tougher than that."

"I thought this was going to be our thing," Alice said with a sniff, as the other riders chatted among themselves. She was horribly aware of Hannah. This was the second time in a row Secret and Alice had disrupted the lesson.

"I think it is!" Angus said. "Secret has the talent. We just need to work on *your* confidence."

It sounded simple, Alice thought, as she clambered back on board.

Then it was Hannah's turn to jump. Barney, her skewbald, was very well schooled and Hannah sat beautifully, tiny in the saddle, her glossy dark ponytail swinging out behind her as she and Barney soared over the jumps and landed in perfect harmony. They were almost guaranteed a place on the team. She'd never seen them put a foot wrong.

When it was her turn to jump again Alice took a deep breath, and this time she managed to jump

the spread perfectly, so at least they ended on a good note. But even when things went right Alice felt the weight of the trials on her shoulders. It had seemed such a good thing to aim for, but what if they – *she* – wasn't good enough?

"Shall we head for a drink in the café?" Amy said as they all warmed down together.

Hannah glanced at her watch. "If I've got time," she said in a superior voice. "I'm meeting the party planner. Shame Angus had to spend so long on *certain* people today." She gave Alice a pointed look.

"Don't be mean," Sam said. "Remember when you first got Barney? You fell off him, like, six times in one lesson."

Hannah glared at him, then she smiled a cool, smug smile. "Whatever. Our relationship is so good now," she purred. "Finn has been amazing. Like really involved, you know? He *totally* gets me." She glanced at Alice as she said the last sentence.

Amy tried to change the conversation. "Party planner?" she said. "Exciting! What are you going to be talking about?"

"Well," Hannah said grandly, as everyone gathered their ponies around her. She reminded Alice of a queen holding court. "You won't recognise the indoor arena! I'm going to keep some of it as a surprise, but expect BIG things. I'm talking ice sculptures, ice rinks, fake snow, the works. Dad's got a band as well as a DJ, and a reporter from *Teen Mag* is coming to cover it. So you'd all better be looking amazing!"

Alice thought back to her own birthday party. A barbecue in one of the farm fields, with the ponies nearby. But she was looking forward to Hannah's party despite the forced invite. Samantha had helped Alice find the most amazing sequinned

material that her dressmaker friend was going to make into a slinky gown. Alice had been into town and found some cheap jewellery and face glitter, and Samantha had shown her how she could pin her hair up. She couldn't wait for Finn to see her all dressed up! Then her face fell. Hannah had said Finn was going with her to the party. But what did that actually mean…?

★

Soon the long cold January was over and, as they entered February and the new show season dawned, the yard became a hub of activity.

Alice and Secret attended a couple more group lessons, and another fun show with mixed results. They managed to come second at the fun show, but in the group lessons Secret was still strong and excitable. Every time Alice thought they'd made progress with their groundwork there would be a moment in a lesson when she felt completely out of

★
★
159
★
★

control. The trials were just round the corner, and she had to decide whether to put them forward for a place in the team. And with both the trials *and* the party on the horizon, Alice felt the pressure starting to build.

Chapter 16

One morning Alice was woken by white light shining through her window. Pulling back her curtains, Alice gasped. It had snowed overnight and Park Farm had been transformed into a winter wonderland!

"School's emailed," her mum called up the stairs. "It's closed. The heating has packed up."

No school! She could spend a whole day in

the yard, Alice thought joyfully. Ella, whose stable door had been left open as usual, stood in the doorway, pulling at her hay net. Secret, on the other hand, rolled with joy in the snow, all four legs off the floor. Encouraged by Secret, Ella took a hesitant step forward and snorted as she buried her muzzle in the snow, before trotting a circle, powder flying and her tail fanned out. She was enjoying it! Alice wished Finn was there to see the ponies play.

"Does it remind you of the Highlands?" Alice asked Fergus, who chuckled.

"This is nothing!" he snorted. "The roads are still fine. You wait until it snows again, then we *might* be in trouble. I can't believe they shut the schools!"

"I'm not complaining!" Alice grinned. And she really wasn't, especially as Finn's school was also closed and he was coming over to see Ella.

They both looked up as a Landrover crunched up the drive: Angus, Finn and Sasha. With a faux-fur hat on top of her mass of blonde hair, Sasha looked like a model, Alice thought, glancing down at her own sludgy green overtrousers.

"Hey, Alice!" Sasha said. "I haven't seen Ella in a while so I wanted to say hello."

A second four-by-four crunched up, driven by Samantha.

"Hello, hello!" Samantha called, waving. "Alice, I've got your dress!"

Samantha enveloped Alice in a hug, before embracing Angus, Sasha and Finn.

"Oh, Alice, Finn!" Samantha said a short while later as Finn proudly showed off Ella. The change in the grey mare was clear to see. Ella's eyes were bright and she was relaxed as she came out to greet the visitors. Secret, on the other side of the fence, whickered lovingly. Then Ella gave a rumbly whicker of delight, looking beyond the group as everyone turned to see who she was welcoming. It was Josephine.

"Hello, girl," Josephine said softly, extending her hand.

"Oh, Josie!" Samantha said in delight. "She seems to love you."

"She's sweet," Alice's mum said with a smile. "Finn has done a great job."

"And Alice," Finn piped up, putting a hand on Alice's arm. Despite the cold Alice could practically feel her skin burning. "But we have Josephine to thank: once we realised Ella liked Secret, Josephine let us move Secret in next door. *That* was the turning point."

"Oh lovely," Samantha said happily. "Ella making friends. And how is Secret coming along?"

Alice smiled. "He's good. He can still be tricky sometimes, but I feel like we're making progress."

Angus, who had been listening to the conversation, turned to Alice. "Look, I know things are up and down for you. But when you and Secret are good you're *really* good. I think you have a chance of making the team. You should try out."

Alice glanced at her mum, who, to her surprise, nodded. "I think you should too, Alice."

So that's that hurdle cleared, Alice thought. Her mum was on side. Alice had fought so hard to go her own way with Secret, and the next steps were down to her.

★

"Shall we ride out? I'll take Lachlan?" Finn asked, once his dad and Sasha had gone.

"In the snow?" Alice said hesitantly.

"Why not?" Finn said. "There's no ice; it's soft powder. So if we stick to the tracks we should be fine."

To Alice's surprise, her mum agreed, as long

as they promised not to leave the farm. Alice felt her excitement grow. She'd seen photos of ponies being ridden in the snow, and now she was going to do it!

Fergus had grown up riding in the snow in Scotland, and so Alice showed Finn something she'd learnt from the older groom. Together they greased up Lachlan's feet so the snow didn't ball up in his hooves. Secret, being unshod, was well equipped for the conditions.

"Now we're really ready to go!" Finn grinned.

Once they were on board the ponies moved easily through the powder. Alice laughed with delight as they climbed up through the fields, taking out her phone and snapping a photo between Secret's ears so she could remember the moment. Then she nearly fell off her saddle as Finn moved in closer, placing an arm round her and turning the phone

around so she could snap a photo of the two of them.

"Cheese!" he grinned good-naturedly, and Alice knew she would keep that photo for ever and ever.

She was still smiling as they reached the top of the farm. The downs beyond looked like a magical landscape, and even though the snow barely covered the grass it still dazzled under the weak winter sun. Alice breathed in, her worries over Hannah and the showjumping team slipping away. If she could just stay in this moment, Secret relaxed and happy, Finn on Lachlan by her side, life would be good.

★

Alice's bubble was burst later that afternoon when Hannah's dad came to collect Finn.

"Hannah was keen that the snow didn't stop you coming to us…" Alice heard Hannah's dad say.

I'll bet, she thought sourly. Still, nothing could

take away their ride that morning, the two of them in the snow on Alice's two favourite ponies. She scrolled through her photos again, smiling to herself.

A little later as Alice cleaned tack, her phone beeped. She frowned as a picture appeared on her screen, and in one second she felt her heart break.

OMG, Amy, check this out! the text read. It was Hannah's number. *Such a special moment!*

It was a photo of Hannah riding Barney and Finn walking beside her on a snow-covered track. Alice recognised the other side of the downs in the photo. Hannah, rosy-cheeked and looking exceptionally pretty, was smiling with happiness at Finn, who had his arm draped over Barney's neck as the pony snuffled at his hand. They looked like the perfect couple. Alice blinked away angry tears. Even though her name probably appeared

next to Amy's in Hannah's phone contacts, she was willing to bet it hadn't been a mistake. Hannah had wanted her to see that photo.

★

"Riding in the snow looked fun," Alice's mum said the next morning as they ate breakfast. "I've been impressed with all the different things you've been doing with Secret recently."

Alice nodded, her mouth full of toast and marmalade, wondering if that was her mum's way of complimenting Angus. Still upset over the photo of Hannah and Finn, she stayed quiet, her eyes red-rimmed after a bad night's sleep, and she lowered her head as she noticed her mum peering at her.

"All OK, Alice?" her mum said gently.

"Yep." Alice feigned cheerfulness but her mum frowned.

"Alice," she said. "If you're worried about the

showjumping, don't be. I'm happy for you to try out, but if you feel it's too much for you…"

Alice shook her head. "I'm fine," she lied. "Probably caught a bit of a cold yesterday."

"I think I might ride Lachlan today," her mum continued, still not looking convinced. "Just around the fields, like you did. It looked so wonderful, and the snow won't be here much longer."

★

"What's up with you?" Finn asked Alice later.

"Nothing," she muttered, concentrating on her tack. She was getting ready to ride out with her mum, and Finn was over to see Ella. She wasn't going to bring up his snowy ride with Hannah. After seeing the photo, she was convinced Finn had fallen for Hannah, and it would hurt too much to have it confirmed. Frowning, Finn took Ella off into the arena.

Her mum led Lachlan out into the yard. With

his shoulder-length mane and striking colouring against the snow, Alice felt a little tug of emotion. She could almost imagine the Highland back up in Scotland, bringing a stag down a snow-covered mountain. That's what Alice loved about the native ponies: you could see the decades of history in them.

Swinging herself up into the saddle, Josephine smiled, and for one second she looked like the teenager Alice had seen in the photos. Soon the ponies were really stepping out, sending up flurries of soft powder as they made their way through the farm.

"Wonderful!" Josephine enthused, taking in the view as they reached the top of the paddocks. It all looked so perfect. But Alice felt very far from perfect. In fact, it felt as though with one problem solved another had been created. She had free rein to go for the showjumping team trials, but she hadn't yet learnt to fully trust Secret, and now with Finn falling for Hannah … what else would go wrong?

Chapter 17

It was the day of Hannah's party *and* the final jumping lesson before the trials. The morning dawned clear, sunny and beautiful. They had a busy day ahead, not least as they were taking three ponies over to Hilltops.

Finn wanted Ella to have experience of schooling in an indoor arena, and so she was going to travel over with Secret and Lachlan. Secret would be taking part in the lesson and as Lachlan was very calm and steady, Josephine had suggested he go along as a companion for Ella. Josephine would collect the ponies and Alice later in the lorry, and bring them back to Park Farm so Alice could get ready for Hannah's party.

Her dress hung up in her window, the sequins catching the winter light. Alice had tried it on the night before, earning a little clap from her mum and dad as she twirled around. It was so unlike anything she'd ever worn, but she couldn't wait to wear it.

Alice's mum had been right about taking Lachlan. The mild-mannered gelding stood patiently on the lorry as Ella nervously boarded, and with Lachlan snuffling her muzzle gently she relaxed as she was tied next to him. Secret bounded up the ramp as he always did, excited about going out.

Hannah was waiting for them as they arrived.

"Thanks for letting us do this, Hannah," Finn said as they unloaded the ponies. Ella was wonderfully calm, a contrast to her arrival at Park Farm.

"Oh, Finny!" Hannah put a hand on his arm. "After all the help you've given me, it's the *least* I can do!" Then she glanced at Alice. "I can't wait until our surprise later!" she said to Finn. "Will you be coming back after you've dropped your ponies off?"

Finn nodded. "Yeah, we'll need a bit of time to prepare. I'll be straight back," he said, and Hannah smiled adoringly at him.

Alice frowned. "What are you doing?" she blurted out and Hannah giggled.

"Oh!" she said. "I'm not giving anything away, but let's just say our entrance will be amazing!"

Alice turned to Finn once Hannah had waltzed off. "Are you going to the party with Hannah?" she asked quietly.

"Well, sort of." Finn looked guilty. "I mean, only because I'm helping her."

"I'm sure it's gone beyond just doing a favour for your dad," Alice snapped, unable to help herself. She didn't care any more; how could he not realise how much Hannah liked him?

"It's not like that. I've just been helping her with her pony," Finn said, but Alice pushed past him, taking Secret and leaving Finn with Ella and Lachlan. She felt very alone, and had a sudden sense of foreboding. Why did everything suddenly feel wrong?

★

Things went from bad to worse once the lesson was underway. Alice, already on edge, was aware of Hannah behind her.

"Let's hope we don't have to sit around for ages *again*," she said loudly, overtaking Alice, who flushed as Secret jogged sideways.

A PONY called SECRET

By the time it was Alice's turn Secret was fizzing over with excitement, and she caught Hannah smirking as she trotted a circle ready for her first jump. Alice clutched nervously at the neck strap as Secret started to canter sideways. As he launched himself over the first three fences, Alice found herself left behind, clinging awkwardly on. By the last fence, she had just about managed to gain control and had one perfect jump, sailing over the filler like Secret had wings in his hooves. But Alice felt like it had been a disaster. She slowed Secret to a walk, leaning over and patting him so no one would see how upset she was. It was dark, she realised, like someone had pulled curtains around the arena.

"Sometimes a bad practice before the real event is a good omen!" Angus said reassuringly, and Alice gave him a weak smile. Doing well at the trials felt like an almost impossible task, but she wanted a place so badly. She wanted her dream with Secret to come true.

Riding back out, it took Alice several seconds to process why it was so dark. Snow was falling thick and fast, and the ground was already covered.

She heard Hannah gasp next to her. "How romantic and perfect for my party!"

"Not if no one can get there," Amy said sensibly. "And how are we going to get our ponies home?"

"Four-by-fours," Hannah replied airily. "Everyone was on the road the other day!"

But Alice knew it wouldn't be that easy for her. With three ponies to collect, her mum would have to bring the lorry, and although they lived nearby, there was a steep hill that would prove almost impossible in the snow. Looking at her phone she saw she'd already missed several calls from her mum. Alice called her back immediately, and her mum answered on the first ring.

"We can't get the ponies home tonight, love," she said at once. "I've already spoken to Hannah's dad and they can stay in the spare stables. I'll come over as soon as I can to collect you, but dad's out in the four-by-four at the moment."

Finn, emerging from the second arena after schooling Ella, blinked away snowflakes from his dark eyelashes. *Ella looks great*, Alice thought briefly. *Happy and relaxed with Lachlan by her side.* Alice passed the phone over to him, and he nodded as her mum filled him in.

"Finn!" Hannah came sauntering over, having put Barney away. "Isn't this exciting?"

"That's not the word I'd use," Finn answered bluntly.

"If you're worried about the horses, don't be!" Hannah laughed. "Dad's got loads of spare stables. They'll be fine."

"But will Ella be OK?" Alice asked, remembering

how Finn had been so against Ella being moved to the equestrian centre.

Finn frowned again. "We have no choice. Hopefully if the gritters are out, the lorry can come tomorrow."

"But the party… All the noise, the lights."

"The stables are nowhere near the school," Hannah said with a frown. "How do you think *our* ponies are going to cope? We're not having fireworks or anything like that."

Finn looked at Alice and nodded. "Ella will have Secret and Lachlan with her. She'll be fine, I'm sure."

But even so Alice heard worry in his voice.

Chapter 18

The snow carried on falling while Finn and Alice settled the horses in. Alice had to admit that although the yard was far busier than her mum's, the stables were lovely, and the three Park Farm ponies had a block at the far end in the quietest spot. Ella immediately started munching at a hay net, taking her cue from Secret and Lachlan on either side of her.

Alice's mum rang with an update. "Dad's still not home; he's been delayed by the snow on the roads. I'm sorry, Al, but I don't think I'm going to be able to get your dress to you in time."

Alice sighed. *There goes my one chance to wear the sequinned dress*, she thought a little sadly. "It's fine, Mum. I'll stay here and keep an eye on the ponies."

A moment later Hannah appeared and pounced on Finn. "We need to be ready to go soon. Loads of people are still coming, so it's all good!"

Then she looked at Alice, her smile fading. "What about you?"

"I'll stay here until my mum comes to get me. I can't get home to change," Alice explained.

Hannah grimaced. "Oh. What will you wear?"

Alice glanced down at her outfit, her faithful navy jods with the seam going at the knee and a wool sweater that had been her dad's until he'd

accidentally shrunk it in the wash.

"This, I guess, unless I borrow Secret's rug," she replied, unable to keep the sarcasm out of her voice.

Hannah made a face. "Your jods?" she said, wrinkling her nose. "Well, your call, but maybe keep out of the way of the photographer."

"I intend to," Alice muttered, still thinking of her sparkly dress hanging up at home.

Hannah lost interest in her, rushing off to have her hair and make-up done, and so Alice sat in the café, watching as four-by-fours started to arrive. She had no idea where Finn was, so she had checked the ponies several times.

As the music started to play and glossy teens wearing incredible winter-themed outfits spilled from vehicles, Alice examined her reflection in a knife. Her hair was pulled back into a top knot, her nose was reddened, her skin pale. *I look dreadful,* she thought miserably. Sipping on her third hot chocolate, she decided to sneak in and watch the start of the party. The hum of music made its way over from the largest indoor arena. It had started to snow again, the flakes dancing in the glow of the fairy lights strung up on the path towards the arena.

Sliding in as inconspicuously as she could, Alice gave a gasp. The indoor arena had been completely transformed. The sand was covered in fake snow, ice sculptures towered up towards the ceiling, and glittering mirror balls hung from every beam. It looked like the sort of party you saw in magazines, Alice thought, and then remembered that it probably would be.

"Alice!" It was Amy, waving madly, dragging Lola and a few other girls over to say hello. There was no escape now, but at least Amy was kind enough not to mention Alice's non-outfit. Everyone

else looked amazing, a blur of sequins and glitter and white fake fur, looking far older and more sophisticated than they did day to day.

Alice spotted Jordan chatting with a girl near the chocolate fountain. *He is quite handsome*, she found herself thinking. *But nothing like Finn*. But where was Finn?

Then the music changed, and an excited buzz filled the arena as a low drumbeat sounded. The lights blacked out and a single spotlight shone on the big double doors as dancers twirled around it.

"This is it!" Alice heard Amy say in an excited voice. "Hannah's big surprise!"

The doors slid open and everyone gasped. Hannah was riding Barney, who had been transformed. He had glitter all over his coat, his mane was plaited up in silver ribbons and he had silver polish on his hooves. *He looks like a Flying Fillies pony*, Alice thought. But it was Hannah, riding bareback, who caught her eye. Dressed in the most amazing silver dress with a low-cut back, her long dark hair loosely curled and flowing over her shoulders, she looked breath-taking. It took Alice a second to realise Barney had another rider. Finn. All in black, his arms were wrapped round Hannah's waist. As they reached the middle of the arena, Finn leapt off and then gestured at Barney, who lowered his head and front legs as though he was bowing. Alice recognised the bow as one of the tricks Finn used in his demonstrations. That must have been what he had been teaching Hannah and Barney.

Reaching up to Hannah, who slid off as gracefully as a ballet dancer into Finn's arms, the two waved to the crowd who broke into applause. Hannah snuggled up to Finn, who placed an arm round her shoulders and smiled down at her, and Alice's vision was blurred by tears.

Pushing her way past the crowds, Alice found a quiet corner, trying to compose herself. The chemistry between Finn and Hannah was only too obvious.

A groom came to collect Barney, who looked thoroughly pleased with himself, as Hannah hugged her friends, her pretty face alight as she introduced Finn to everyone. He was surrounded by people, a novelty among the normal pony club crowd.

A few minutes later Finn appeared behind Alice, and she hurriedly patted her eyes so he couldn't tell she'd been crying.

"Alice!" Finn sounded pleased to see her, but Alice just stared blankly at him.

"What's up?" Looking confused, Finn moved towards her and Alice folded her arms.

"If you don't know now, Finn, then you never *will* know!" Alice blurted out before she could stop herself.

"What are you talking about?" Finn said as he followed Alice's gaze to Hannah, who was surrounded by friends, every now and again tossing her glossy hair over her shoulder and gazing at Finn. A look of recognition dawned on Finn's face.

"Alice, are you mad about *Hannah*?"

"Mad?" Alice gave a short laugh. "Why would I be mad? I can't stop who you go out with."

Finn shook his head. "I know I've spent loads of time with her," he said, "but it was all for today … for the party!"

"It doesn't seem that way to me!" Alice snapped. And with that she bolted, leaving behind the music, the lights and the glamour. The cold air hit her hot face with a rush, and reaching in her pocket for her phone she dialled home. It was still snowing, and Alice felt her tears mingle with the flakes.

A PONY called SECRET

"Mum, is Dad back?" she said, trying to keep her voice steady. "Please can you come and get me?"

"Of course," her mum answered. "He just got home at last. Give me fifteen minutes."

Taking a deep breath, Alice decided to go and wait with the three ponies instead. Lachlan, Secret and Ella were the only company she needed right now.

As she crossed the yard, the music growing quieter, Alice sniffed. What a disastrous day. She felt as though she'd not only lost Finn, but her chance to gain a place in the showjumping team, after their bad performance in the lesson.

As she rounded the corner to where the Park Farm ponies were, Alice frowned. There was a group of teens outside and panic among the ponies. Secret was standing rigid in his box, eyes searching, as Lachlan gave a startled whinny. Alice gasped. Ella's door was open.

Alice turned on the group furiously. "What happened? Where's the grey pony?"

A blond boy in a tuxedo shrugged. "We were only being nice," he drawled. "We wanted to give the ponies a pat. The grey pony seemed a bit shy, so we opened her door to give her a polo, and she scarpered."

"What do you mean 'she *scarpered*'?" Alice shouted, full of worry and anger.

"Don't get so *stressy*," one of the girls snapped back. She had a faux-fur jacket flung over her shoulders and was wearing a white floor-length dress. "We're not used to horses. Hannah said they were all friendly…"

"You idiots! You stupid idiots!"

Alice sprinted as fast as she could back to the arena. She needed help. She pushed open the door and shoved her way through the crowd until she reached Finn, who was with Hannah. She was

standing close to him, nestled into his shoulder as she threw her head back, laughing at something. Alice didn't care. She grabbed Finn's arm and he gave her a look of surprise.

"It's Ella, she's out," she said in an urgent voice. Finn started to follow Alice, but Hannah pulled him back.

"What's the problem?" she said in a friendly voice, but her eyes were glinting dangerously. "If one of the ponies has got out, they'll only be in a field. Alice can catch her. Help yourself to a feed scoop if you need it, Alice." She waved a dismissive arm.

Finn pulled his arm free. "You have no idea what you're talking about," he said to Hannah, who narrowed her eyes at his words. "I'm coming, Alice." Taking her hand he pushed his way through the party and raced across the yard. The teenagers had left, but Lachlan and Secret were still pacing back and forth.

"Right," Finn said. "Hopefully she's in a paddock. You go left, I'll go right."

Both set off at a run. The snow was still falling, giving an air of serenity, the music from the party barely noticeable. Running around the track of the paddocks, calling desperately, Alice gave a start as she noticed hoof prints leading to an outer fence, beyond which lay a path to the downs, the route Alice was planning to take if she rode over in the summer. The prints had left long scrapes in the snow, as if whoever had left them had made several attempts to jump, veering off at the last second. But one set of prints led out over the other side. Ella must have jumped, and she was long gone, her prints disappearing off into the vast white unknown.

Chapter 19

Finn was pacing up and down on the phone to his dad as Alice's mum's car pulled into the yard. Alice quickly filled her mum in as Finn came over, looking grim.

"Dad's on his way," he said, eyes searching the vast expanse of white land beyond the equestrian centre. His dark hair was flattened against his head, snowflakes catching his high cheekbones.

"Ok, here's what we'll do," Josephine said firmly. "I suggest Alice and I ride out on to the downs. Secret knows Ella, maybe if he whinnies, she'll hear us."

"But I've only got Secret's tack," Alice said in a worried voice.

"I'll ride Lachlan in a head collar, and I'll use a couple of lead ropes as reins," her mum replied in a brisk business-like voice. "Finn, you look on the road with your dad as soon as he gets here. If you go out of here, turn left and left again, follow the road up a mile, there's a five-bar gate from the downs on to the main road. Look for the horse sign. We'll go up on horseback and try to cover as much ground as possible."

Finn was wavering, looking hesitantly at Alice.

"I want to come with you," he said, frowning. "Why don't I ride Lachlan?"

Alice's mum shook her head. "No," she said. "I

grew up here. I know those downs. Lachlan will look after us." She gave the big Highland a pat. "Go with your dad."

Alice quickly tacked Secret up, as Finn legged her mum up on to Lachlan's broad back and tied Ella's head collar on to Secret's saddle. If it hadn't been for the circumstances, it could have been a fantastic adventure. They were on the best transport for the harsh conditions, two true native ponies, sure-footed and bred to cope with the snow.

It was easy at first to follow Ella's hoof prints. But as they rode on, the tracks became harder and harder to make out, and Alice started to panic.

"Where could she be, Mum?"

"She's got to tire soon," her mum answered, but she sounded worried too.

It had finally stopped snowing. The air was freezing, the snow sparkling in the light of the moon, bathing the downs in silver. Alice shuddered. She couldn't bear to think of Ella out alone on such a bitter night; surely she wouldn't survive.

"We've got to find her soon," Alice's mum said, but she didn't sound confident now.

Alice looked at her mum, who was biting her lower lip, eyes constantly searching the horizon. "You really like her, don't you?" she said.

"I do," her mum said softly. "I really do. She has a way of getting right under your skin. I honestly don't think I've felt that for a horse since Lachlan." She reached down and stroked Lachlan's thick mane. "Some horses just grab you."

Alice knew exactly what her mum meant. She'd had the most amazing bond with Honey, her first pony, and then when Secret had come along he had stood out to her in a whole yard of ponies. It was like they were supposed to find each other.

"Like Blue," Alice said, not thinking, and for one

second her mum closed her eyes.

"Just like Blue," she said. "He really was one in a million." Then she smiled, looking wistful. "I'm glad you found the scrapbook," she continued to Alice's surprise. "I was going to show you, one day. Seeing you on Secret reminds me so much of my relationship with Blue. That's why, even though I'll never forget what happened to Blue, I agreed to let you have the lessons with Angus."

"Finn says he feels truly awful, that he was only trying to help you." Alice felt brave enough to say it, and her mum sighed.

"I'm sure," she said quietly. "But that doesn't change what happened. And Blue paid the price."

They had reached the top road. Angus's Landrover was parked on the verge, hazard lights flashing. He and Finn were both out of the vehicle, shining torches up and down the road.

"Any sign?" he called out to Alice and her mum.

"No," Josephine called back in a despondent voice. "Nothing."

Suddenly Secret's head lifted, his ears pricked. Letting out a piercing whinny he danced on the spot, desperate to run.

"What is it, boy?"

Alice gathered her reins as Secret let out another whinny, his eyes searching for something.

"I think he knows something." Angus and Finn had appeared, hope back in their faces, and Alice knew what she had to do. She just had to hope Secret didn't bolt. She dropped her reins, and took a deep breath. "Show us where she is, boy," she murmered. "I trust you."

"I'll keep Lachlan beside you," her mum said. "Come on!"

Secret had already turned, jogging, in the direction of the road, whinnying over and over. The reply was so faint Alice wasn't sure if she

was imagining things at first as Secret surged forward. Then she blinked, wondering if her eyes were playing tricks on her as a grey pony trotted up towards them in the centre of the road, sides heaving, splatters of blood a stark contrast against her white coat.

"Ella!" Alice's mum cried, and at the sound of her voice the mare lifted her head and gave a quivering whinny.

"We've got to get her off the road," Angus said as Alice and Josephine rode through the gate and on to the verge. The verge was so wide that they didn't need to go on the road itself, but it was still unnerving with nothing between them and the tarmac.

Ella seemed disoriented and unwilling to be caught, but did at least scramble up on to the verge. A four-by-four crawled slowly past, headlights illuminating the snow.

"Right," Josephine said firmly. "Alice, you get behind her, and I'll go in front. We need to block her in somehow. Give me her head collar, I'll get her."

"I'll stop her going back on to the road," Finn said, running in between Alice and Josephine, clapping his hands and trying to encourage Ella towards Lachlan, closing the space between them. They were so nearly there, Alice thought. If they could just get close enough, then her mum could reach up and slip a rope round Ella's neck.

"Easy, girl, easy." Josephine was talking to Ella in a low voice as she neared her, and it seemed to snap the little mare out of her trance. Slowly she edged her way towards Lachlan, who whickered softly at her. The kindly gelding stood firm as Ella stumbled towards him. Now she was closer, it was clear to see her cuts were just scratches. Slipping off Lachlan's back, Josephine extended her hand.

She was so close. There was nothing more Alice could do; she watched as her mum carefully placed a lead rope over Ella's neck. Ella visibly relaxed. She was safe.

"Thank goodness," Finn said, now next to Alice. "Let's take Secret over to her."

They started to cross the short distance towards her mum, who had fastened the head collar on to Ella.

Secret heard it first, ears pricked as he lifted his head.

The thump of a stereo, the whine of an engine, the sound of tyres hitting snow at speed. Looking up, Alice saw headlights. Even with Angus's hazard lights flashing, the four-by-four made no effort to slow down, as the vehicle tore through the snow, sending flurries of powder into the air, before it seemed to hit an icy patch and began swerving all over the road.

It all happened so fast.

The four-by-four skidded as the driver desperately tried to regain control. Coming off the road and hitting the verge, the vehicle slowed on the banked-up snow, but continued to spin round.

"Mum!"

"Alice!"

Alice became aware of Finn grabbing Secret's reins and her arm, and being pulled aside, falling and stumbling in the snow. Flanked by Finn, her face pressed into his chest and Secret squealing in fright, Alice cried out as the four-by-four skidded past them on the verge, missing them by centimetres.

Josephine, clutching both Ella and Lachlan's lead ropes, was caught in the headlights and screamed as she desperately tried to turn the exhausted and disoriented Ella, and Lachlan gave a whicker of alarm.

Alice lunged forward, but she was too slow. The car was going to hit them, she realised, and there was nothing she could do.

Lachlan, the biggest, kindest horse on the yard didn't move. Standing firm, his eyes trusting and loyal, his broad body took the weight of the four-by-four as the vehicle came to a stop with a sickening thud. Josephine and Ella, sheltered by the solid Highland, were untouched. Lachlan had saved them.

Chapter 20

Angus was the quickest. Already beside Josephine, he took Ella's lead rope as Josephine stood frozen, still clutching Lachlan's makeshift reins.

Apart from a small mark on the bumper, the four-by-four looked OK, so Lachlan must surely be fine, Alice thought desperately.

The driver opened the door, a mix of anger and guilt on his face. "What were you doing—" he

started to say before Angus shot him a look of such fury that he quickly shut up.

"You were going way too fast, *that's* why you came off the road and on to the verge," Angus hissed. "Stay exactly where you are."

Another Landrover had stopped, driven by a man Alice recognised as a local farmer. Pulling on to the opposite verge, he jumped out, running and sliding across to help.

"I saw it all," he called. "This idiot's been doing circles in one of my fields so I followed him. I've rung the police."

Alice felt like she was watching a TV drama. Blankets were thrown over Ella and Lachlan, who remained strangely still. With a dreadful sickening feeling in her stomach, Alice realised there was something seriously wrong with Lachlan's left hind leg, the one that had taken the brunt of the impact. He wasn't putting it on the ground and stood instead on three legs. Josephine was still clutching his lead rope, her face white, clearly in shock.

"Josie," Angus said softly, "listen to me. Lachlan's seriously hurt. Don't try to move him, just stay at his head and comfort him."

Josephine nodded, touching Lachlan's big gentle face, running her hands through his forelock. Angus moved quietly round, carefully inspecting the big Highland's body, and then winced. Blood had started to pool against the white snow.

Slipping off Secret, Alice was aware of Finn's hand closing over hers. She felt unsteady as they made their way towards Ella and Lachlan. Ella was calm, her head lowered, as Finn took the lead rope, before turning to Alice.

"We need to call your vet," he said, his voice low and urgent. "Do you have the number?"

Alice nodded, passing her phone over numbly.

Her eyes were fixed on Lachlan's leg.

Put your foot down, she thought desperately. *Put your leg on the ground and let us see you're OK. Please, Lachie.*

But Lachlan, his head lowered, his sides heaving, kept his leg in the air. A feeling of dread swept over Alice and a flashback of Honey's accident swam before her eyes, her beautiful mare who'd suffered a heart attack when jumping, both Alice and Honey falling, everything going black. That had been a cold winter's day too, Alice realised. She felt the same helplessness, knowing something was terribly wrong and that the world was about to be shattered.

A few minutes later Harriet the vet pulled up in her four-by-four. She'd been the Smalleys' vet for as long as Alice could remember – and was a real friend of the yard. A shadow fell across Harriet's face as she looked at Lachlan, and it told Alice everything she needed to know.

Josephine held Lachlan's big head between her hands, before running a hand down his wide forehead, arranging the forelock and calming him. Lachlan was sweating now, clearly in pain, and his eyes pleaded with his mistress to help him.

Moving quickly and quietly, Harriet assessed Lachlan. Then she turned to Alice's mum, placing a hand on her arm. Her face was solemn.

"I'm sorry, Josephine," she said kindly, a note of sadness in her voice. She had looked after the gentle pony ever since he had arrived from Scotland as a youngster. "Lachie's got a catastrophic injury: an open tibial fracture, and possibly some other breaks as well." She shook her head. "He won't get better from this. There's nothing we can do; we wouldn't be able to repair the fractures, even in a hospital."

"No, please, Harriet," Josephine pleaded. "Make him better. Angus, tell her, tell her to try, just like we did with Blue. I know he won't be ridden again, but please, just save him."

Angus shook his head, his face sombre. "I'm so sorry, Josie," he said quietly.

Alice looked down and realised she was still gripping Finn's hand tightly. "Not Lachlan," she whispered. "Please, not Lachlan."

A police Landrover pulled up next to the ponies. The police officer spoke quietly with Harriet as Josephine started to sob into Lachlan's mane. Finn and Alice moved closer, Secret and Ella following solemnly behind.

"Josie," Angus said softly. "You need to be brave, for Lachlan. Try to hold your tears for now. He needs to know you're there for him."

Alice's mum bit her lip and gave a deep shuddering breath and began talking in a low voice to Lachlan. Alice could tell her mum's heart was breaking.

Moving quietly, Harriet spoke to the police officer again, who nodded and quickly set up a screen around the ponies. The farmer, watching from his vehicle, took his flat cap off, holding it to his chest as Harriet prepared a syringe.

"This first one will just sedate him, calm him down, and then the second one will put him to sleep," the vet explained. "It will be peaceful, I promise. It's the kindest thing we can do for him. Lachlan will just go to sleep, with no more pain."

Josephine, now gripping Angus's hand, nodded. Alice could see her mum was making a heroic effort not to cry in front of Lachlan. Alice choked back a sob of her own.

It was all so quick. Just a few moments later the big Highland was on the ground, his shattered leg finally giving way as he lay heavily on his side.

Lachlan breathed deeply, once, then twice. Then there was silence.

The vet knelt down, listening to where Lachlan's strong, proud heart had once beaten, and gave a small nod.

"He's gone," she said softly.

Chapter 21

Only then did Josephine dissolve into sobs, kneeling beside her beloved pony, tears falling on his thick mane. Angus knelt beside her, still holding her hand. Alice clamped a hand to her mouth, her legs buckling, before she felt Finn's strong arms round her. Her throat burned with a sob, her cheeks were wet with tears, freezing in the evening chill.

"Oh, Alice," Finn said in a choked voice, tears falling down his face. "I'm so sorry. But I'm here for you. I'm *always* here for you."

Alice felt a nudge on her shoulder. It was Secret. Alice leaned on him, breathing in his warm, familiar scent. The little pony stood quietly, as if sensing his wise old friend was gone.

Finn turned back to Alice. "We should go before they come to collect Lachie," he said in a low voice. "I think it will upset Secret and Ella too much."

"I'm not going back to Hilltops!" Alice said, suddenly panicked, and Finn shook his head.

"We're not too far from your house," he said. "Let's go straight back to Park Farm."

"How?" Alice said tearfully.

"You ride Secret. I'll lead Ella," Finn said. "It's not far if we go the direct route. We rode here last summer, didn't we?"

Alice's mum was pale, leaning on Angus as he

held Lachlan's head collar. The sight of the worn leather head collar that had hung in the tack room for the whole of Alice's life was too much for her and she collapsed against Secret's side, sobbing. Finn placed an arm round her again.

"How can he not be coming home?" Alice cried, and Finn shook his head.

"He's not," he said, his voice cracking. "I'm so sorry."

Secret gave Alice a nudge, and she refocused. Finn was right: they had to get the ponies home and safe, however hard it was. She was going to have to put all her trust in Secret again, to lead them home.

"Oh, Lachie." Wiping her eyes, Alice gave a deep, shuddering breath. It had long stopped snowing, the sky twinkling with a thousand stars, now joined by one more, the brightest one in the sky. Alice knelt beside her mum, trembling as

she placed a hand on Lachlan's neck. He was still warm. How could he be gone?

She threw her arms around her mum, who looked completely shell-shocked.

"You go," Angus said quietly. "I'll look after your mum. And I'll make sure Lachlan's taken care of."

Nodding, Alice kissed Lachlan's neck, breathing in his familiar sweet smell, holding the silken strands of his mane between her fingers as she closed her eyes, picturing him thundering around an arena, magnificent and the wisest of all the ponies. "Goodbye, sweetheart."

Secret gave a small whicker, as if saying his own goodbye as Alice rode him back through the gate and on to the downs. Ella followed quietly as Secret ploughed through the snow, which was over his knees in places. The moon was bright as they followed the bridleway signs back down, an owl swooping and hooting overhead and Finn's torch catching the eye of a fox or a rabbit every so often. Apart from the crunch of snow between the ponies' feet, it was completely silent.

Without realising it, tears continued to roll down Alice's cheeks as she thought of Lachlan lying peacefully in the snow. "I've never seen a horse put to sleep before," Alice said, choking back a sob and placing her arms round Secret, feeling him solid and warm beneath her. He constantly amazed her. He could be so wilful and headstrong, but now he was calmly leading them home through the snow.

"Will Ella be OK?" she asked Finn who was now in step beside her.

Finn nodded. "Look at her now," he said, placing a hand on her neck. "Trusting us and Secret to guide her home. She was terrified, but she came to us up there on the road; she came to us for help. This night might be the making of her."

Alice thought back to the group at the party.

A PONY called SECRET

By opening Ella's stable door their actions had set off a chain of events that had resulted in Lachlan's death. The party seemed a distant memory now.

"Finn, about earlier…" she started to say, and Finn held up a hand, as if he knew what she was about to say.

"Don't," he said. "I know how it looked with Hannah, but I really thought she just wanted lessons. But then she called me her boyfriend when I met her school friends." He looked annoyed. "Boyfriend! *Please*, she's not my type at all. Especially after tonight."

Alice thought about the way Hannah had looked at Finn as they rode into the party.

"I *was* enjoying helping her with Barney. And she's fun. But go out with her?" Finn shook his head and looked straight at Alice. "I can't imagine her turning up to a party in old jods and still looking beautiful, riding to the rescue of a pony in the snow. *If* I had a type … that would be it."

Alice felt her heart thudding under her jacket. She couldn't believe what Finn had just said. His words danced around her head.

Moments later they arrived back at Park Farm, and everything looked calm and peaceful.

Angus was back already, helping Fergus hang up hay nets ready for Ella and Secret. Fergus had tears running down his cheeks and Alice gave him a hug. She knew how much he had loved Lachlan.

"Your mum's gone inside with your dad," Angus said quietly, gesturing towards the house. "Harriet's on her way here to check Ella and Secret."

Ella and Secret rolled and rolled in their deep beds, then they were both wrapped up in warm wool rugs. Harriet pulled into the yard a few minutes later. She said that both ponies seemed fine, and recommended that they have a few

days' rest and gentle walking out.

Fergus looked at his phone and frowned. "The local news says the main road is now completely blocked."

Angus looked at Finn. "We'll stay here tonight," he said. "I'd rather stay and keep an eye on Ella anyway, just in case. I'll let Sasha know."

Finn nodded.

Just then, Alice's mum came across the yard bundled up in a blanket. Her face was pale and her eyes were red but she gave a small smile when she saw Ella and Secret tucked up safely. Angus quickly filled her in on the state of the roads and his plan to watch over Ella. Josephine frowned, and for one brief second, Alice wondered what her mum was going to say.

"You can't stay out here all night," she said. "We'll do it in shifts. There are two beds made up in the groom's flat."

Angus smiled gratefully. "Thanks, Josie. And I'm so, so sorry. For everything," he said.

Alice's mum looked straight at him. "It's OK," she said quietly. "It wasn't your fault. Thank you. Thank you for helping me keep Lachlan calm, right to the end."

Angus nodded, and put his hand on Josephine's arm for the briefest of moments. "It's the least I could do," he said quietly.

★

They worked as a team that night, keeping watch over the ponies. When she wasn't watching Secret and Ella Alice tried to sleep, but despite being exhausted she couldn't switch off. As she and her mum sat in the stables together, her mum smiled sadly.

"It won't be the same without him," she said softly. "I should have ridden him more. I'd forgotten how wonderful it was to hack out."

Ella stirred, twitching in her sleep. She was standing up, hind leg resting.

"Lachlan saved her," Alice's mum said, giving a small smile. "He was a hero, right to the end."

★

It seemed wrong, Alice thought, as a pink sun rose over the snow, that the morning should dawn so beautifully without Lachlan. She was stiff with tiredness as she and her mum and dad nursed mugs of coffee at the kitchen table.

There was a tentative knock on the door. "We're off," Angus called. "Sasha needs our help at home and the road is back open."

"Thank you," Alice's mum said quietly.

There was a moment's pause, before Angus reached into his pocket.

"You might not want this now," he said, pulling out a small drawstring bag, "but I asked Harriet to cut a section of Lachlan's mane."

He passed over the bag and Alice's mum opened it, her eyes filling with tears as she gently touched the lock of hair.

"He'll always be with us, Mum," Alice said. "He's always going to be part of Park Farm."

"Just like Blue, up in the top paddock." Josephine looked up at Angus, and they shared a small sad smile.

Chapter 22

A week passed and Alice missed Lachlan so much it physically hurt. The stables just weren't the same without him.

Alice's mum had thrown herself into working with Ella. Just as Finn had predicted, Ella's flight in the snow had given her a newfound confidence. Alice's mum smiled properly for the first time since Lachlan had died as Ella wandered outside her stable, greeting Secret over the fence with a low whinny.

Then her smile faded. "I'll miss her when she goes back to Angus's yard. The new stables are almost finished so she won't be with us for much longer." She sighed and then looked thoughtfully at Alice.

"Anyway, it's the team trials next week," she said. "You and Secret should go for it. We need something positive to focus on."

★

"Your mum phoned last night to talk through the team jumping with my dad," Finn told Alice a few days later.

"I know," Alice said with a frown. "It's a shame it took Lachlan's death for them to speak to each other again."

Finn nodded and then smiled at Alice. One of his rare, brilliant smiles. "So, what do you say to

trying out?"

Alice realised she didn't care any more about making a fool of herself. Secret adored jumping, so they may as well go for it. If it all went wrong, then they could always try again another time. Alice knew she could trust Secret.

She grinned. "Let's do it!"

★

The weather had warmed up a few degrees for the showjumping trials, which were to be held indoors. Secret felt fresh, with a spring in his step. Alice took a deep breath. Secret had proved again and again that when it really mattered she could trust him. Then she had an image of Lachlan: kind, wise and reassuring. She had to do this, for Secret and Lachlan.

As she and her mum waited with Secret, a familiar pony appeared next to them. Barney, ridden by Hannah. Alice noticed Hannah's cheeks

225

redden. She stared at her, wondering what she was going to say.

"I'm sorry," Hannah blurted out. "Dad gave that group the biggest telling-off the next day when we heard what happened. They're *never* coming to my house again! Banned for life!" For a second, she seemed full of herself again, then she dropped her head. "I really am sorry about Lachlan," she said quietly.

"It's OK." And Alice meant it: she didn't blame Hannah for her friends' stupid behaviour. Although she couldn't quite forget Hannah being so dismissive of Ella's escape.

Hannah headed off, holding Barney's reins as she flung her arms round a handsome boy Alice vaguely recognised from her party. And although Alice couldn't be certain she was sure Hannah was watching Finn over the boy's shoulder as she did so. For a second, Alice's eyes met Finn's, and

he rolled his eyes and grinned at her. She smiled, feeling the unspoken connection between them. And then it was Alice and Secret's turn to jump.

The trials were simple: a course of fences about seventy centimetres high. Alice knew Secret could easily jump the height; it was the bits in between that she was worried about. The standard was high, with most people jumping clear with the odd run-out or refusal.

It was nearly Alice's turn. She noticed her mum and Angus watching together, with her mum smiling at something Angus was saying.

Secret gave an ear-splitting whinny as he spooked at his own reflection in the mirrors, jogging and prancing. Circling and talking to him, just as Finn did with Ella, Alice aimed him at the first fence, taking care to sit up and not hold on to his mouth. Launching himself back, Secret took off from over two strides out, clearing the jump by miles.

Alice gripped hard on to the neck strap. Somehow she managed to right herself in her saddle, searching for her missing stirrup, as she aimed for the next fence.

Again, Secret over-jumped it but then he started to calm down. He cleared the rest of the course in style, and then, delighted with himself, did three full laps of the arena before Alice could pull him up. She gave a huge grin. During the second part of the course they'd felt in perfect unison, as if Secret could read her mind and she his. Adrenalin was fizzing through her as she finally slowed him to a walk.

June Darby chuckled. "Well done. He certainly won't have any trouble in the jump-offs!"

Alice slid off Secret, praising him. She'd done her best, and it was a clear round. Now it was up to June and Angus to make their choice. Once everyone had jumped, and the ponies were back

in their lorries, June clapped her hands and called everyone to the arena.

"Excellent work!" she said, looking around her. "We've got the first interbranch competition coming up in June, and we want to select four riders to go on for further lessons in preparation. We've decided the four riders we want to go forward are Jordan, Sam, Hannah and ... Becky."

Alice's stomach slumped. Secret had jumped so beautifully, and she'd allowed her hopes to be raised. But she'd done her best – and Secret had done his best – and that's all that mattered.

"I'm proud of you, Alice," her mum said warmly as they walked back to the lorry. "That was a real achievement."

Then June Darby called them back. "Hang on!" she said cheerfully. "I wanted to talk to you about the team. Alice, would you be happy to be a reserve?"

Alice's mouth fell open. A reserve! It wasn't a team place, but it was enough, for now. She was part of something, something she and Secret both loved.

"Yes, please!"

Alice looked over at Finn, who mouthed *"You did it!"*, and felt like jumping for joy. She'd done it: the first part of her new journey with Secret. It would be hard juggling the training and helping her mum, but she was going to make it work.

Angus appeared next to her. "Lots to work on," he said with a grin, "but I think you both have so much potential. You've just got to strike the right balance between his enthusiasm and his talent, and you need to trust him, and yourself!"

Alice's mum nodded and started to discuss the training lessons and dates of upcoming events with Angus.

Alice smiled at Finn, who winked back.

Chapter 23

Alice and Secret's triumph at the pony club trials had lifted the mood of the yard, although Alice still felt a lump in her throat when she passed Lachlan's empty stable, his rug still hanging over his feed manger. One afternoon, her mum pulled all the old photographs out and they looked through them together, smiling at how Lachlan's colouring had changed over the years, admiring him in the ring as a three-year-old and in later years under the Olympia spotlight.

"You're doing the right thing with Secret, you know," Alice's mum said unexpectedly, gazing at a particularly beautiful headshot. "Just enjoying him, and being the best you can be at what you really love."

Alice nodded. She wished there was some way she could make her mum feel better. Then her mind started to tick.

She rushed out into the yard, where Finn had just arrived to see Ella. "Finn?" she asked as he looked at her curiously. "Can I come and talk to your dad?"

★

"*Sell* Ella to you?"

Alice was sitting in the kitchen of Rookham Manor. She shook her head. "Not to *me*," she explained. "To my mum. Or at least offer her, to

see if mum wants to buy her."

Angus frowned. "But Ella won't make a show pony, not with her scar. She wouldn't be much use to your mum, or her business. She might hack one day, or even do a little dressage, but that would be all. We were just going to keep her for a pet."

"I know, but Mum is really enjoying her time with her. They have a special partnership," Alice insisted. "Can you at least ask her if she'd be interested…"

Angus frowned. "It was never my intention to rescue her to sell her on," he said. "I know she'd have a brilliant life at your yard, Alice, but I'm not going to sell her. I'm sorry."

A few days later it was time for Ella to leave Park Farm. The snow had started to melt, a hint of spring on its way. Josephine was standing at Ella's side, her hand resting on her neck. Alice thought her mum had tears in her eyes.

"I'll see you soon," Alice whispered, giving Ella a kiss. She'd miss her, and she knew Secret would too. When Finn and Angus's Landrover appeared without the trailer, Alice frowned. How were they planning on taking Ella home?

"What's this?" Josephine said, obviously thinking the same thing. "Are you coming back later with the trailer?"

Angus smiled. "We can," he explained. "But I wanted to ask you something first." He took a step towards Josephine. "Would you consider keeping Ella...? That is, if I were to give her to you, would you be happy to have her?"

"You want to *give* Ella to me?" Josephine repeated, looking stunned.

"Only if you want her," Angus explained. "Alice asked me a few days ago if I'd consider selling her, but I refused. I didn't pay anything for her, so it

wouldn't have been right. But Ella needs a home where she can have a one-to-one relationship with someone. She'd have a wonderful life with you."

There was a long pause while Josephine gazed at Ella. Alice held her breath, crossing her fingers in her coat pocket. Had she done the right thing, asking Angus? Maybe her mum *had* wanted to send Ella back.

Finally Josephine turned to them, her eyes shining. "Lachlan saved her," she said in a choked voice. "She'll always have a home here. I'd be honoured to have her, thank you."

★

"What a winter!"

Finn and Alice were finally able to hack out again, Alice on Secret and Finn on Archie, who was back for the spring. The snow had long since melted, and the first flowers poked their heads up from the ground.

"Tell me about it!"

"Is your mum enjoying having Ella?" Finn asked as they turned back to the yard.

Alice smiled. "Yes," she replied. "They're really helping each other."

"Horses can do that," Finn said. "Ella was obviously meant to be with your mum." He smiled at Alice. "And how's the prep going for the area competitions?"

"Good," Alice nodded. "Your dad's given me some more exercises to do at home and there's quite a few lessons coming up. It's quite nice being reserve. I can take part without the pressure of the *actual* competition. I've just got to learn to manage Secret's excitement at the start."

Finn chuckled. "He wouldn't be Secret without a bit of quirk." Then he looked thoughtful. "But he's proved that when it counts you can rely on him."

"Funnily enough, that's exactly what I thought

when I did my trial," Alice remarked. "How when I really need him he never lets me down."

Finn smiled. "Pony of a lifetime."

A stab of pain hit Alice. Blue, and then Lachlan, had been her mum's special ponies, and before Secret Alice had Honey. And yet everyone was moving forward. Josephine and Angus had healed their rift, and Alice and Finn were friends again. Ella was flourishing with Josephine's love. And then there was Secret.

Brave, cheeky Secret, leading Ella to safety through the snow and jumping like he had wings on his feet. Alice knew they had a long way to go, but she was determined to enjoy their journey together. She'd never felt so proud of Secret, her beloved red pony who surprised her every single day.

Acknowledgements

Thank you to the wonderful team at Nosy Crow, in particular Kirsty for all her expert help and guidance and Nic for her amazing design skills and for producing the most beautiful covers. A huge thank you to my lovely editor Sarah who totally 'got' Finn and Alice from the start and has been amazing to work with. And thanks to the whole team at Nosy Crow who support the books so brilliantly from start to finish!

I must thank Julian Radburn, our wonderful vet from Damory Veterinary Clinic. His advice really helped with writing the hardest scene I've ever had to write!

Thanks also to Sarah Weston for all her amazing advice and information. Sarah absolutely helped me to understand why Ella was the way she was.

Special thanks to Jolie Darton, owner of Butler – our beautiful cover star. Jolie made sure Butler looked like a superstar ready for his photo shoot!

Finally, writing pony books really is the best job in the world and I must thank my husband Clive who supports me every step of the way. And of course my daughter Lara, who keeps me smiling and whose love for ponies mirrors my own.